RIDE THE HIGH LINES

Because of his speed with a gun, they called Ash Colter 'The Gunsmoke Legend'. But he put his gun away, figuring to buy some land and raise horses. To do that he needed money, so he agreed to undertake one last, dangerous assignment — to track down the notorious outlaw John Kidd. One bloody confrontation piled atop another and, in the end, Colter had to face the unsettling fact that he had more in common with Kidd than he thought.

Books by Matt Logan
in the Linford Western Library:

COFFIN CREEK

MATT LOGAN

RIDE THE HIGH LINES

Complete and Unabridged

LINFORD
Leicester

First published in Great Britain in 1995 by
Robert Hale Limited
London

First Linford Edition
published 1998
by arrangement with
Robert Hale Limited
London

British Library CIP Data

Logan, Matt
    Ride the high lines.—Large print ed.—
Linford western library
    1. Western stories
    2. Large type books
    I. Title
    823.9'14 [F]

    ISBN 0–7089–5278–X

Published by
F. A. Thorpe (Publishing) Ltd.
Anstey, Leicestershire

Set by Words & Graphics Ltd.
Anstey, Leicestershire
Printed and bound in Great Britain by
T. J. International Ltd., Padstow, Cornwall

This one is for Shirley Day —
because her production values are
second to none!

1

GEORGE Frederick Baxter, manager of the Denver branch of the Territorial Bank of Colorado, settled himself into his big, button-studded leather chair and said, "Well then, Mr Childs — and how may we be of assistance?"

It was exactly ten o'clock on the morning of April 2nd 1877, and the man sitting in the visitor's chair on the other side of the big, polished desk considered the question for some time before forming his reply. He had bright blue eyes, a largish nose and a square, firm-looking jaw, and he appeared somewhat out of place in his steel-grey suit and matching string tie. He fiddled with the narrow-brimmed hat in his big hands as he tried to find a way to begin.

"Well, uh . . . "

Baxter judged him to be somewhere in his early twenties — which, to be perfectly frank, meant that Childs did not fall into the range of people with whom he normally conducted business. George Frederick Baxter was a man of high commerce, and older, wealthier men who occupied positions of influence and power were more to his liking.

He himself was a tall, spare man, dressed elegantly — if a little funereally — in a well-tailored black suit and sober grey cravat. Now just three years away from retirement, he had a face that was pale and pinched, with oily black hair that was brushed back from a high forehead and carefully moulded to the shape of his skull.

His office was the office of a successful man. The oak-panelled walls were hung with paintings of the bank's board members, and panoramas of the open-range cattle and silver industries that had made Colorado great. Leatherbound books stood to attention on sturdy shelves in one of two recesses, and a well-stocked drinks cabinet occupied the other. When Baxter shifted in his chair, the leather upholstery gave out an impatient squeak that sounded loud in the confines of the room.

Baxter did not suffer fools gladly, and this fellow Childs had struck him immediately as a man who could win prizes for his foolery. For more than a week now, Childs had been pestering his secretary for an appointment. Stubbornly he had refused to be put off. The fellow simply would not take no for an answer.

A fastidious man in both appearance and speech, Baxter winced at the double negative. But this Childs really *had* been persistent, no two ways about it. So finally the bank manager had given his secretary instructions to go ahead and make an appointment. A five-minute one. And now, here was Childs. Edgy, fumbling Childs.

"I don't wish to appear discourteous,

sir," Baxter said, pointedly taking out his pocket watch and checking the time. "But . . . "

The chain that looped from one vest pocket to the other cost more than most of his clerks made in a year. But then, why shouldn't Baxter enjoy the finer things of life? In his view, he had earned them, having started at the bottom and worked — some said *toadied* — his way up through the ranks.

Eyebrows raised, Baxter squinted at the note on his blotter. "You told my secretary that you had to see me on a matter of great importance," he prompted.

Childs nodded. He had a mop of thick flaxen hair and a fringe that fell across his forehead in a clumsy spill. "As indeed I do, Mr Baxter," he responded at last, inching his way ever closer to the edge of his chair. Dropping his voice, he said, "You see, I have chanced upon certain . . . information . . . that I feel you should know."

Baxter said boredly, "Oh?"

"Yes. Information that concerns your bank, Mr Baxter."

Baxter frowned. "My — ? What about my bank, sir?"

Very deliberately Childs said, "It's going to be robbed, Mr Baxter."

Baxter sat up straight. *Robbed*. It was the one word that no bank manager liked to hear, much less contemplate. He looked closer at Childs, trying to decide whether or not the fellow was telling the truth. After all, who *was* this Childs? Baxter knew nothing about him, save that he had about him the air of a fool.

"Is this your idea of a joke, Mr Childs?" he asked at length.

Childs looked right back at him, his blue eyes innocuous and earnest, and shook his head.

"Then how did you come by such information?"

"That," said Childs, with a shrug, "is neither here nor there. But I can assure you that a plan to rob your bank of not less than twenty thousand dollars is most definitely afoot."

Now it was Baxter's turn to squirm, for there was something in Childs' quiet manner that compelled belief. Still, he was reluctant to accept the fact that his bank, *his* bank, had become the target of robbers. For not once, in almost thirty-eight years in the banking business, had he or his staff ever been intimidated by outlaws.

Oh, it *happened*, of course. It happened all the *time* in this lawless half of the country. But to other people. And other banks.

Baxter had always been proud of his reputation. It was both unequalled and unblemished. If at all possible he wanted to keep it that way. And, if this young man's information was correct, then he must pass it along to the authorities without delay. But first —

"Just who *are* you, Mr Childs?" he enquired curiously.

"You're probably better off not knowing that," Childs replied mysteriously.

Baxter frowned. What the devil was that supposed to mean? He opened his mouth to insist upon an explanation, but then fell silent again. Perhaps the fellow worked for the bank in some secret, investigatory capacity. Perhaps he was answerable only to the board of directors, his very existence a closely-guarded secret.

He changed tack. "Well, sir, do you know *when* this . . . attempt . . . is going to be made?"

Childs nodded again and said, "This very morning."

Now Baxter's eyes bugged. This *morning*! If Childs was right, they would have to move fast indeed. He cursed himself for not having seen the man right at the very start. If only he's *known*! At least then they would have had more time to alert the authorities.

But then Baxter pulled himself together. To berate himself now was futile. How was he to know the purpose of Childs' visit? He glanced across the

7

desk at Childs again, then stood up and came around to join him. "I will have to send someone for the police," he said. "You will have to tell them what you have told me."

"No police," Childs said softly.

Baxter pulled up short. "But . . . the police *must* be notified, Mr Childs."

Childs stood up, too. "I think *not*," he said, more firmly this time.

The everyday sounds of the bank at work outside drifted in to fill the silence, and Baxter was suddenly struck by a feeling of loneliness and isolation, a realisation that he was entirely at the mercy of his young visitor, and that he had been from the moment that Childs had first walked in.

He groaned weakly. Only now, when it was too late, did he understand how Childs had come by his information — because it was he *himself* who intended to rob the bank!

"I — "

"Not a sound, Baxter."

Childs reached slowly into his pocket

and Baxter, his whole morning suddenly capsized by this new and unexpected turn of events, followed his movements with fevered eyes, reaching out to grasp the edge of the desk and steady his watery legs.

But a moment later Baxter gave a grunt of surprise, for instead of the gun he had been expecting Childs to produce, the young man only took a phial of pale yellow liquid from his pocket and held it high in his right hand.

With sweat pebbling his forehead now, Baxter's eyes travelled up the length of Childs' arm to the phial in his grip. His twitching eyebrows lowered into a frown. A question formed on his lips but he couldn't get it out.

Guessing the nature of the question, Childs volunteered an answer. "It's a compound of glycerol, nitric acid and sulphuric acid," he explained. "It's called trinitroglycerin. Perhaps you've heard of it. It is extremely unstable. The slightest jolt — " and here he shook the phial, making Baxter cringe, " — and it will explode. This bank, all the people in it — half of this entire *block*, in fact — will be history."

Baxter clenched the edge of the desk so hard that he almost splintered his fingernails. His eyelids fluttered and his eyes went up into his head. *T-Trinitroglycerin*, he thought. *Trinitroglycerin* . . . Oh God, yes . . . yes . . . he'd heard of it. It *was* unstable, just as this man said.

But surely, if Childs used it, he would kill himself along with everyone else! Baxter opened his eyes, a sudden, absurd sense of triumph making him feel quite light-headed.

To his surprise, however he found Childs only smiling at him, a crazy light having entered his eyes. Reading his mind, Childs said, "Do you think I give a damn for my life, if I can't get my hands on that money?" He backed away from the other man and raised the phial a little higher. "I'll be honest with you, Baxter — I've half a mind to go ahead and blow us all up anyway."

Baxter's eyelids fluttered some more. *Oh my God*, he thought. *The man is a lunatic.* He cleared his throat and said in a strangulated voice, "Now . . . now l-listen to me, Childs. There is nothing to be gained from using that l-liquid. Just . . . just k-keep calm, man, and . . . and we'll work something out."

"Indeed we will," Childs replied. "You will call your chief cashier in here and tell him to fetch twenty thousand dollars from the vault."

"*W-what?* I couldn't — "

"You could. And you'd better. Who is your most important client?"

Baxter had to think a moment. After a while he croaked, "Th-The Argent Mining Corporation."

"All right. If your chief cashier asks, you'll tell him that I have just delivered a bank draft from Argent Mining for funds that are needed as a matter of urgency. And you had better give a convincing performance, you old goat, because if he suspects that something is wrong, I won't hesitate to use this."

Again Baxter winced. "You c-can't hope to get away with it," he husked.

Childs made another careless gesture with the unpredictable compound. "For the sake of every man, woman and child within forty yards of this office, you had better hope that I do," he replied, fixing Baxter with a gimlet eye. "Now wipe your face and get back behind your desk, then ring for your man. And remember, Baxter — just one little jolt . . . " And again he gave the deadly phial a twitch that made the bank manager shudder.

Baxter took a handkerchief from his pocket, flipped it open and wiped his face. His heart was pounding so hard that it was making him feel nauseous. They both retook their seats, Childs slipping the phial back into his pocket and crossing his legs, and then Baxter reached a finger towards the button on his desk.

Before he pressed it, however, he

fixed Childs with as stern an eye as he could manage under the circumstances. "I'll see you hunted down for this," he promised. "I swear it."

"I'd be surprised if you didn't at least try," Childs answered urbanely. "But as pleasant as it is to sit here and swap threats with you, Baxter . . . " And here, Childs had the effrontery to reach a watch from his own vest pocket and consult the time.

Baxter cursed under his breath. The nerve of the fellow! Then he pressed the button, and a moment later there came a discreet knock at the pebbled-glass door. Baxter said in an uncertain voice, "Come."

The chief cashier entered the room. He was of average height and build, with glasses and a small, neatly-trimmed goatee beard. He closed the door quietly behind him and came to stand on one side of the bank manager and his visitor.

"You wanted to see me, Mr Baxter?" he said.

Baxter had about him a wheezy, half-throttled look. He was starting to sweat again as he nodded and replied, "Yes, Carson. I . . . This gentleman has just delivered an urgent draft for twenty thousand dollars from Argent Mining. I would be obliged if you would fetch that sum from the vault."

Without batting an eye, Carson said, "Certainly, sir. Do you have the draft there?"

Baxter stared at him a moment, then nodded. "Yes. But, uh . . . there are one or two things I want to discuss with Mr Childs here about it before I . . . p-pass it through for processing."

Carson inclined his head. "Very good, sir." He turned to Childs. "How would you like the money, Mr Childs?"

"Any way it comes, Mr Carson," Childs replied cheerily. "A mixture. I leave it to your discretion." He reached down and offered up the black leather bag he had brought in with him. "Here — pack the money into this, if you would be so kind."

Carson eyed him oddly, as a frown ploughed up the hitherto-smooth slope of his forehead. "Very good, Mr Childs. I'll . . . I'll attend to it at once."

He left the room.

Baxter wiped his face again. "Give it up now, man," he said desperately. "I implore you. Look, just . . . just walk out of here right now and I'll give you my word that I won't pursue the matter. We'll just write it off as . . . as an aberration."

Abruptly Childs sat forward. "That's a strange word to use," he snapped bleakly. "You're not saying that I'm *crazy*, I hope."

"No! N-no, of course not . . . "

The young bank robber sat back again. "God help you if you are," he warned ominously. He took the phial from his pocket again and held it up between thumb and forefinger so that Baxter could see the deadly yellow liquid it contained. "Because if you're as tired of all this as I am, you've only

15

got to say the word . . . "

"No . . . p-please . . . "

Childs pinned him with wild, daredevil eyes. "It won't hurt, Baxter, if that's what's worrying you. My word on it. It'll be so quick, you won't know much about it. Just one — little — shake of this bottle and . . . *BOOM!*"

And to prove his point, he gave the phial another jog.

Baxter went crimson in his desperation. "No! No . . . d-don't do that." His limbs went limp, and his seat seemed almost to swallow him up as he flopped back. How could he deal with a man like this, a madman who appeared equally content to live as to die? The simple answer was that he couldn't. God help him, his life was in this maniac's hands.

"Just . . . just take the money and go," he croaked finally.

The bank robber slipped the phial back into his pocket. "That's the spirit," he commended, his mood brightening again. "Now, cheer up, man. I'm only

16

taking twenty thousand."

They waited in silence after that, with the wall-clock ticking ponderously and a puddle of dusty sunlight crawling slowly across the burgundy-coloured carpet, and street-sounds filtering in from Lawrence and East 40th. Baxter mopped his face again. Childs merely sat humming, apparently unflustered by his precarious position.

At last there came another tap at the office door, and Baxter said, "Come."

The chief cashier, Carson, came back into the room with Childs' bag in one hand and a thick ledger in the other. He set the bag down beside Childs and said, "Perhaps you'd like to check the money before you sign for it, sir?"

The bank robber peered up at him. "I don't think there's any need for that," he replied airily. "You strike me as an honest man, Mr Carson, and since you are the chief cashier, may I assume that you have something of a reputation for accuracy?"

17

Carson preened. "Well, I like to *think* so, sir."

"Then your word is good enough for me."

He reached for the ledger and helped himself to one of the pens in Baxter's stand. He read the most recent entry, muttered, "Uh-huh," and then signed his name with a flourish.

Baxter watched him. Childs was outnumbered now, two to one. Together he and Carson could probably wrestle the fellow to the ground and thwart the robbery. But when Carson glanced at him with one raised eyebrow, his expression clearly saying what an odd gentleman he considered this Mr Childs to be, Baxter only gave a helpless little shrug.

No, they dare not risk a struggle with Childs, not if that trinitroglycerin was as volatile as he had been warned. Why, the slightest jar and —

Baxter's breath caught in his throat. The consequences did not bear thinking about.

Childs handed the ledger back to Carson and said, "Thank you." Then he popped the pen back into the stand, stood up, clapped his hat on to his head, picked up the bag and thrust out his right hand. "Well," he said, "it's been an experience meeting you, Mr Baxter. I hope this will be the start of a long and happy relationship."

Baxter glared at him across the desk, furious that such an unbalanced upstart should add insult to injury. But what was he to do about it? There was nothing. Because he had the safety of his staff and clients, as well as those workers in the adjoining buildings and even the people going about their business in the street outside to consider, and it was an awesome, debilitating responsibility.

His mouth thinned down to an ill-tempered line and grudgingly he got to his feet and shook the other man's big, calloused hand.

"Perhaps you will be so kind as to see me out?" Childs enquired casually.

Baxter nodded, not trusting himself to speak immediately. "Of . . . of course."

Clearing his throat discreetly, Carson said, "The bank draft, sir?"

"*Later*," rasped Baxter.

The three of them headed for the door. Carson opened it and stood to one side while the bank manager and his strange but oddly likeable visitor filed out. They went through a flap in the counter and ambled down through the echoing, busy bank, an imposing structure with lavish wood panelling, gleaming black and white floor tiles and a high, vaulted ceiling.

As they headed for the sunshiny windows and double doors at the far end, Childs said in an undertone, "You've done very well, Baxter. My compliments."

"It's not too late to give it up," Baxter responded. "Don't . . . don't take this the wrong way, man, but you . . . you're obviously unwell. *Here*." He tapped his forehead with two fingers.

"You need help. I could arrange such help if . . . if only you would give this business up."

"I'm touched by your concern," Childs said mockingly as he hefted the bag. "But I predict that *this* will give me all the help I need."

He dropped back to allow Baxter to open one of the doors for him, and then they walked out on to the concrete sidewalk, into the hive of activity that was Larimer Street.

The city was all telegraph poles and trolley-cars, men in suits and women in bustled finery. Childs went across to a big chestnut horse standing at the rack and hooked his bag over the saddlehorn, then untied the reins and prepared to climb aboard. For a moment it looked as if Baxter's nerve was about to break, so he came back over, reached into his pocket and brought the phial out again, and the sight of it alone was sufficient to stifle any alarm he might have been about to raise.

No more than three or four feet separated them now. It was about the closest they had been since this whole sorry episode had started. But still Childs kept his voice low, so as not to alert any of the people hurrying past.

"Not a word of this until I'm out of here, Baxter," he said. "If there is any sign of pursuit, you may be sure that I will throw this bottle into the first sizeable crowd I see. Men, women, infants . . . Once the smoke has cleared, you will see for yourself just how devastating this pretty potion of mine can be. But it needn't come to that, if you co-operate."

Baxter gulped. He had not the faintest shadow of doubt that Childs meant what he said. The man was insane, and wholly unpredictable. And certainly *he*, Baxter, could not live with such an act of carnage on his conscience.

But . . .

Suddenly he frowned. Out here in the bright, crisp, early spring sunshine, he was getting his clearest look yet at Childs, quite literally seeing him in a new light.

Except that this man's name *wasn't* Childs. Baxter realised that now.

Recognition dawned at last, and again he cursed himself for a fool. Of course! This was a face he should have known instantly, for he had seen it often enough in the past, on Wanted notices.

Childs saw something in the bank manager's eyes that he didn't like the look of, and his own expression tightened. Baxter, meanwhile, was bringing up one accusing finger, his eyes widening, his normally-pale expression turning positively apoplectic as he told himself that this man wasn't a lunatic at all, but a cold, calculating, iron-nerved outlaw.

"You . . . you're *John Kidd!*" he whispered. Then louder: "You're the outlaw *John — Kidd!*"

Childs — Kidd — shook his head in a mixture of irritation and regret.

"Didn't I tell you you were better off not knowing that?" he asked.

And so saying, he spun around, shoved through the crowd and threw himself up onto his horse.

For one instant then, the two men locked stares. A second later Childs/Kidd broke the spell that held them both frozen in time.

He brought his right arm up and back, and —

— *and hurled the phial straight at Baxter.*

Baxter screamed and brought one of his own arms up, but he was way too slow. For even as Kidd hauled his mount away from the rack, and the animal reared up onto its hind legs, even as he kicked his heels into its flanks and roared, *"Gitalongthere!"*, the phial was spinning end over end towards him.

Desperately Baxter tried to turn and throw himself back into the relative safety of the bank, but it was too late for that. The phial struck him on the chest, the thin glass shattered, and the trinitroglycerin splashed all down his smart black suit.

Only dimly did the fact of Kidd's escape register with him. As you may understand, Baxter had other, more pressing matters to occupy him just then. He screamed in sheer, blind panic, lost his balance, fell flat on his backside there in the middle of the sidewalk and yelled, "For God's sake, *help* me, someone! I've been doused in high explosive! Fetch the police! *Quickly!*"

A small crowd gathered. As one, the curious passers-by looked at him as if he were mad. Whether one of them actually did as he begged, or whether the policemen arrived under their own steam, drawn by his hoarse, hysterical screams, he would never know. But within a very short space of time, a pair of copper badges pushed through the crowd and came to stand over him with hands on hips.

All of this was still some years

before the Denver Police Department decided to issue its men with blue serge uniforms and chalk-white gloves, of course, so these two were dressed in civilian clothes and they carried handguns in high-slung cartridge belts.

Giving him a very queer look, one of them tugged at his moustache and said, "It's Mr Baxter, isn't it? From the bank?"

Baxter resisted the temptation to nod, or show any other sign of physical excitement, for fear of setting off the liquid that was still dribbling sluggishly down his front.

"For God's sake!" he hissed, spraying spittle in a wide trajectory. "The b-bank has just been *robbed*, man, and I've been covered in l–liquid explosive!"

Hearing that, a murmur went through the crowd, and by mutual consent they all stepped back a pace. The policemen, however, only glanced meaningfully at each other. Something intuitive passed between them, and then the one with the big moustache nodded sagely and, addressing Baxter, said discreetly, "Pull yourself together now, Mr Baxter. You're drunk."

Outraged, Baxter said, "*What?*"

The policemen made to grab him by the arms and drag him to his feet, but he shied away from them, fearing the consequences of any sudden movement. "*No!*" he yelped. "For the love of Christ, officers, you've got to get me out of this jacket first! He threw a phial of liquid explosive at me! I could go up at any moment if we're not careful!"

"Come on now, Baxter," said the second policeman, losing his patience. "Take hold of yourself, man. You're causing a disturbance here. And you're showing yourself up something shameful, man in your position."

"Don't touch me!" Baxter snapped. "And how *dare* you accuse me of being drunk!"

"Well," said the first copper badge, sniffing theatrically as he settled into a crouch over the fallen man. "If you're not drunk . . . " and here he lowered his voice, " . . . it's for sure that you've pissed in your pants."

Scandalised now, Baxter opened his mouth to demand the fellow's name and badge number, but before he could say anything at all, he too suddenly caught the acrid, acidy stench of urine on the cool morning breeze, and frowned.

Fearing the worst, he glanced down at himself and thought, *Oh no. Don't tell me . . .*

Cautiously he tucked his chin into his chest, the better to examine the damp patch on his jacket. Gently, he took hold of one lapel and brought it up to his nose.

The smell was unmistakable.

He closed his eyes for a moment, and his shoulders slumped tiredly. The policemen watched him suspiciously. Then —

Baxter fairly leapt back up onto his feet, his face a picture of rage as shattered glass splintered still further under the soles of his shoes. *Trinitroglycerin be damned!* he thought. Pushing past the surprised policemen, he jabbed a finger down the street, vainly searching for the man in the steel-grey suit. *"Get that man!"* he thundered, even though 'that man' was no longer there for the getting. "He just robbed the bank!"

Now the policemen swapped another look, and one of them said, as if this was the first he'd heard of it, "Robbed the bank, you say?"

"Yes!" screamed Baxter. "Robbed the *bank*! Of twenty thousand dollars!"

And that much was certainly true . . . But while George Frederick Baxter later gave a remarkably detailed account of the robbery first to the police, then to his superiors at the Territorial Bank of Colorado, and finally to the bank's insurers, it was only good common sense that made him ever-so-slightly revise some of the events of that early April morning.

After all, Baxter was only three years

away from retirement. And he had his reputation to consider. And surely, *no* man wants to confess that he has been gypped out of twenty thousand dollars by a perfectly sane maniac who threatened him with nothing more explosive than seven fluid ounces of still-warm urine?

2

ONCE the drink finally took hold of him, my friend Jack Page would often declare, "Half of what they say about me is lies . . . and the other half just isn't true!"

Sometimes he would throw his head back and laugh about it, for he could be a man of great humour when he chose to be. But at other times I would see his handsome face darken and his brows meet and his lips press so tightly together that the blood would squeeze from them, and I would realise that it was also a source of great frustration to him.

As his companion for some ten years, I think I understood that frustration. For all his faults — and there were plenty of those — Jack truly was a remarkable man, as history has since confirmed. He was the kind of person we all aspire to be: larger than life and — superficially, at least — the embodiment of all that is good.

In his time, Jack had been a sharpshooter, a stagecoach driver, a guide, a lawman . . . and he excelled at every profession he chose to follow. As his reputation grew, however, he also became an actor, and the role he was forced to play again and again was that of Jack Page . . . the public *perception* of Jack Page, that was.

Too late, Jack found that he was living his life not for himself, but rather for his adoring public, a public that accepted all of the lies avidly and without question, and yet would not countenance the simple fact that he was, above all else, just a man.

Yes, I flatter myself to think that I understood my complex partner, and I have written at great length elsewhere of those heady years we spent in each other's company. In that previous account I tried to set straight all of the other misconceptions that had grown up around him, for never have I known another man who had so many falsehoods and fabrications and downright lies written about him.

Unless, of course, I include myself.

Of necessity I recalled much of my own personal history in that earlier memoir: so, mindful of repetition, I will merely summarise it here. My name is Ash Colter, and I was born on a small farm in Iowa in 1848. My formative years were largely unremarkable, and eventually I grew into a tall, softly-spoken boy with sky-blue eyes and a retiring personality. Before I was much past my seventeenth birthday, however, I was left all alone in the world, my father having been killed at Vicksburg in the summer of 1863, and my mother having contracted some form of lung fever that killed her within a month of war's end.

Since my mother had taken us both away from the farm shortly after my father died, I led a fairly nomadic childhood. But eventually I came into the employ of the celebrated Overland Mail Company, and was able to set down roots as a chore boy and stablehand at the Snake River stagecoach station in the great state of Nebraska.

It was here, in 1867, that I first met Jack Page — 'Hair Trigger Jack', as people took to calling him many years later, when they finally began to tire of his killing ways. But that is neither here nor there, for Jack does not really feature in this narrative, save that it was under his tutelage that I learned to use a gun, and went from chore boy to scout, from Indian-fighter to United States Marshal and, finally, to town tamer.

I recounted all of this in that earlier book, which my publisher saw fit to issue under the title *Gunsmoke Legend*. I did not, however, include any references to my subsequent encounters with the outlaw John Kidd.

To be frank, I have conflicting views on that period of my life, and would as soon put it behind me altogether. But my wife tells me that I should do for John what I did for Jack: that is, to present a true account of the facts and thus set straight all of those lies and half-truths that have proliferated since he left these shores all those years ago.

There is, however, another reason for once again setting pen to paper, and I cannot think of it even now without turning my eyes up to the frame hanging over the desk here in my den.

The frame contains that rarest of all examples of United States paper currency, the ten thousand dollar bill. Not one day has passed in all the years since I first put it up there that I have not looked at it and remembered the circumstances of how it came into my possession and — yes — that I have actually *smiled* at some of the memories it recalls to mind.

This is my other reason for writing the history you now have before you.

Purely and simply because I *owe* it to John Kidd.

Here, then, is my story. His story. *Our* story.

★ ★ ★

It began shortly after I resigned my position as deputy marshal of Yellow Creek, that wild and woolly gold town up in the Black Hills country of what we used to call Dakota Territory. Those were violent, unsettled times, and I can say with some confidence that everything you may have read about the place is probably true. It was a latter-day Sodom, and the greed and brutality I witnessed there turned my stomach so much that in the end, I could hardly leave it quickly enough.

You must realise from the outset that I had fallen into my footloose, gun-swift life entirely by chance. It had never been my desire to ride and kill for a living. I had spent so much of my life with no place to truly call home that all I really craved now was peace, a few acres of land, a wife and, perhaps, a family.

It took my stay in Yellow Creek to realise that I had worn my double-action Adams .442 long enough, and now I determined that the time had come to renounce the gun and make a new life for myself elsewhere.

I knew, however, that if I were to become a man of land and property, I must have money. My salary as deputy marshal of Yellow Creek had been generous, to say the least — two hundred and fifty dollars a month, plus fifty per cent of whatever fines I could collect — but it was nowhere near enough for my purpose, which was to ride south and buy up some good, grass-rich land and establish a horse ranch.

I would have to earn some more money before I could truly call myself my own man.

Not so very long before, I had received the offer of a job from a Mr Simon Black, who was then president of the Cattlemen's Association of Colorado. Although he had not specified its nature, I could guess from the salary he was offering that it would be no easy task. Still, with no more promising avenue open to me, I wired back a response, saying that I would be pleased to at least meet him, and gave him an approximate date for my arrival at Fort Wray, where the Association had its headquarters.

I left the wiles and vices of Yellow Creek behind me in the autumn of 1877, hoping also that I would be leaving all of the violence of that previous existence there as well.

I wasn't.

I will not trouble you with a detailed account of my journey, save to say that it was long and arduous, covering as it did some two hundred miles, down across the hilly terrain of western Nebraska and thence onto the fine, open range country of northeastern Colorado. By the time I began my final push to Fort Wray, autumn was already giving way to winter. The days were growing shorter and duller, and low cloud was piling in from the north to blot out the sun so that each succeeding day was grey and windswept and chilly.

I reached my destination on a brisk October afternoon and turned my dun-coloured mustang into one of the livery stables that could always be found on the outskirts of such a town.

Fort Wray itself had started life as a civilian post, and had remained thus until the Army took it over just after the war. It was a durable edifice of log and adobe construction that overlooked the swift-flowing South Platte River. The town of the same name had spread out from the fort into a somewhat haphazard metropolis served admirably by both the Union Pacific railroad and Wells Fargo.

With my horse stabled, I hung my saddlebags over one shoulder and went in search of a hotel. It occurred to me then, as I walked through streets of brick and timber, past off-duty soldiers, businessmen, cowboys and women, that all I possessed was in those saddlebags. Everything I had amassed over the nine and twenty years of my life.

It came to me, in a moment of self-pity, that I did not have much to show for myself. I was almost thirty — a span which, in those days was considered middle-aged — and yet I had no real friends, no family, no acquaintances even, and precious few prospects. I had money in the bank, of course, and also my horse. But it was a poor show, and no denying.

I found a hotel and paid for a room. The desk clerk gave me a register to sign, and when he saw my name he whistled, studied me closer and finally summoned up the courage to ask if I was *the* Ash Colter. I should have anticipated such a question, for it is not conceit to say that my own reputation had grown alongside that of my more famous companion, merely a statement of fact.

"I am *an* Ash Colter," I replied, my tone making plain the fact that I had no wish to pursue the topic any further.

After that I was given a key, and I took my luggage — such as it was — up to my room. Now that I was here, my most immediate duty was to locate the whereabouts of this Simon Black and let him know that I had finally arrived. I went back downstairs and asked for directions to his office.

The clerk still hadn't recovered from the shock of having *the* Ash Colter staying at his hotel, and he treated me with all the deference another man might bestow upon a saint.

I had seen such a paradoxical reaction many times before, of course, and yet I still could not understand it. To my mind, a man who made his way with a gun, a man who killed or wounded or clubbed other men in order to enforce justice or, sometimes, simply his own will, was to be reviled. I had always been of the opinion that there must be better, less violent ways to uphold the law or win arguments.

And yet both my erstwhile companion and I who had killed or wounded or clubbed other men with a hideous regularity in the course of our adventures — had always been treated with the utmost respect: more, in fact, as if we were visiting gods.

But I digress.

Once I had my directions, I stepped back out into the street. The wind was raw and blustery. It sliced through the thin material of my black suit like the sharpest Comanche skinning knife. With hunched shoulders, and my left hand clapped atop my hat to hold it in place, I set off in search of my destination.

The Cattlemen's Association conducted its business from a suite of offices above the premises of the local newspaper, the Fort Wray *Advocate*, and was situated in the central, commercial district of the town. I reached it by means of a flight of stairs affixed to the side of the building, knocked at the door I found at the top, then went inside.

A clerk, who had been poring over a stack of papers behind a huge, cumbersome-looking desk, recognised my name when I spoke it, and said that while he knew something of the nature of the job for which I had been summoned, there was no-one in authority presently available to see me and explain it further. In the end we left it that he would contact me at my hotel when he had arranged a time for Mr Black to see me.

I left the office, closed the door behind me, descended the staircase and paused for a moment on the busy street to button my jacket against what I could sense was a coming squall.

It was then that I noticed a man standing on the opposite sidewalk, watching me.

At first I gave him only a cursory glance, for I was not completely sure that I was, in fact, the sole object of his scrutiny. I was mildly surprised when he made no attempt to look away or otherwise disguise his appraisal, however, and that made me study him closer.

He was younger than me, as near as I could judge, still in his early twenties. He wore a big black hat tilted low over one ear and forward, so that the brim threw a shadow down over his face. The hat was a beauty, as I recall, an eye-catching Buckeye Stetson. But the rest of his apparel — a plain hunting shirt beneath a short brown jacket, the ubiquitous cuffed Levis and spur-hung boots — was less remarkable. Only his sidearm, which he wore braced against his right hipbone in a knotted-down shellbelt, was worthy of further comment, for it was as well-kept as the hat, and the care that had been lavished on the weapon stirred more than a little disquiet within me.

Something in the fellow's basic manner — his belligerent stance, perhaps, or the brazen, and some might say impudent way in which he sized me up — also worried me, for I had spent enough years plying my rough trade to recognise a troublemaker when I saw one.

For a moment we just looked at each other as wagon traffic rattled by between us. I did not know him. He was not familiar to me at all, and I was certain we had never met before, no matter how briefly.

Putting him from my mind, I set off along the street. I had reached the end of my journey, made my presence in town known to my potential employer, and now I decided to find a restaurant and have something to eat. As you can imagine, I had grown heartily sick of my own feeble attempts at cooking whilst on the trail, and now I was looking forward to enjoying the more accomplished labours of another.

I did not know Fort Wray, so I just started off in the direction of the sinking sun and soon came to a section of the town that had long-since been given over to the pleasures of the constant, if transient, cowboy community. Before long I could not easily count the number of saloons and gaming houses that lined both sides of the muddy thoroughfare. A veritable forest of gaily-painted shingles assailed my eyes: MUSIC HALL, KENO, RAMSEY'S OPERA HOUSE, BILLIARDS, SILVER MOON SALOON — it was a world within a world, and because it offered anonymity, I liked it there.

I found an eaterie that looked to be well-patronised and went inside. I ordered a meal and, as I sat waiting for it to arrive, remembered the parallel I had drawn earlier, about the way Jack and I had always been treated more as gods.

It was true. And, in a way, perhaps we *were* gods. After all, did we not have the power over life and death, however unwelcome and frankly abhorrent I myself might find it? All of my life I had wanted only to set a good example, not a murderous one. And yet Fate had seen fit to set me on a course I was determined to change.

I thought about every act of violence and suffering I had been forced to witness in the previous ten years. It was something I did often, something I could not *help* doing. Every single act of barbarism had killed something inside *me*, too, had left me feeling tainted. But as of now, all that was in the past.

The food came and it was good. I cleaned my plate, paid my tab and left the restaurant half an hour later. In the distance the sky had turned an ominous slate grey, and heavy clouds seemed to boil as they gathered and marched doggedly on towards the town in their path.

I had gone no more than five or six yards when suddenly I heard a voice call my name, and someone grabbed hold of my sleeve and tugged me around. Caught unawares, I had

47

no option but to turn and face my aggressor.

As I completed my pivot, I was in no way surprised to find the tall, belligerent-looking man who had been watching me earlier.

At once I was on my guard, for there was something about the fellow that reeked of trouble, quite apart from the bullish way he had accosted me. I got a better look at the face under the stiff, curled brim of his black Buckeye. His cheeks were full and his nose was small but of the type some call Roman. A heavy moustache obscured his upper lip and curled down to below the corners of his somewhat pouting mouth, and below the mouth his face just slid straight down into his neck, with hardly any chin to speak of.

He gave me his bleak appraisal again. The thumb of his left hand was hooked into his shellbelt, and his right hung loose at his side, his wrist constantly brushing against the grips of his Colt.

At last he said, "You're Colter? *Ash* Colter?"

I had a very bad feeling about him, but knew better than to show it. Trying to sound reasonable and even friendly, I said, "I'm Colter."

"Jack Page's partner?" he pressed, as if he wanted to be absolutely sure of my identity.

I nodded carefully, aware now that a few passers-by were breaking stride to glance around at us, for he did not believe in moderating his tone at all, this one. His lips curled disdainfully and he said, "You don't look like much to me. I was expecting something more."

"Do I know you?" I asked.

He shook his head *no*, but satisfied as to who I was, he spread his feet a little and bent his right arm at the elbow, to bring his hand that much closer to the butt of his gun.

I frowned. "Just what do you think you're playing at?"

He said, "I'm *not* playing."

And he flexed his fingers expectantly.

I had known what was coming all along, of course — or if not exactly *known* it, at least suspected quite strongly that this encounter would turn ugly sooner rather than later. My heart began to beat slightly faster, my breathing to grow more shallow, my throat to dry up and turn scratchy. It had always been that way for me. Some men talk of the pleasure that comes before a kill. I had only ever known this far less palatable reaction.

Narrowing my gaze at him, I said, "Have I ever wronged you, son?"

He said, "No."

"Has Jack?"

Again: "No."

"Then why have you come looking for a fight?" I asked.

A brief, edgy smile tugged at the line of his mouth, and made his moustache stir momentarily. "Don't you know?"

I knew. Lord, he wasn't the first of his kind I had come across, and neither was he the last. In essence he was a nobody looking to become a somebody. He had no skills to speak of, save an ability to use a sixgun. And he genuinely believed that the best way he could make his name was to gun down an even bigger name and add that man's reputation to his own.

I looked at him. He was more of a boy than a man, and not only in his physical appearance. I looked into his eyes. They were sharp and tricky. And yet if you looked deeper, you could also see an almost painful naivete in them. He was doubtless poorly-educated, and he knew little of real life. He wanted wealth and fame but he didn't want to work for it, he didn't have the patience for that, he just wanted the rewards but not the hard work that came *before* the rewards.

I knew that if he hadn't challenged me, he would have challenged somebody else eventually. It was just my bad luck and his even greater misfortune to have heard — probably from the hotel clerk — that I was in town.

51

He was an accident waiting to happen, and I did not want to be the man who taught him the final, irreversible lesson of his folly. But what if I had underestimated him, that he really knew *how* to use that gun he kept so well? What if it was *my* life we were measuring here, on this crowded street in Fort Wray, Colorado?

I said, "I have no argument with you, son. You go your way, and I'll go mine."

I began to turn away from him and he said, "You stay right where you are, you son of a bitch!"

Again he reached out for me. I felt his right hand come down hard on my shoulder and shrugged him off, turned back to him and hit him in the face.

The blow did not carry as much force as it could have, but still it rocked him backwards. He fell off the sidewalk and spilled into the muddy street, his lip split, his face a mask of fury. I stabbed a finger at him and told him to forget about all of this and go on his way. I had not wanted to hurt him, but perhaps my blow might knock some sense into him.

I turned away from him again. My stomach felt so taut that it was as if my intestines were being wrung dry. He yelled my name, but still I kept walking, feeling the eyes of the passers-by shuttling between the two of us now, just waiting for the inevitable to happen.

"*Colter!*" he yelled.

I kept walking.

"No man turns his back on Dick Mills, damn you!" he screamed.

One more pace, one more, one more . . .

"*Colter!*" he screeched.

My pulses racing, I kept walking away from him, hating the idea that all the people in the street would think that I was a coward for retreating this way, but knowing that it was the price I must pay if I were to avoid the killing I so despised.

"*Colter!*" yelled this Mills. "Colter,

your father was a cur! Do you hear me? He was a scrap-eating, mangy-coated *dog*!"

My steps faltered, but still I continued away from him.

"And your mother!" he cried. "She was naught but a whore!"

I stopped suddenly and just stood there, buffeted by the blustery wind. I did not care to see my parents bad-mouthed by anyone, for whatever reason, and for a moment then I nearly turned around and gave the fellow exactly what he wanted, a gunfight. But at the same time I knew why he was saying these things. He was trying to goad me into obliging him, and I would not fall for it.

I took another pace, heard Mills scream something that was distorted by his rage, and in the very next moment someone else, one of those passers-by who had halted on the other side of the street, called out in a desperate voice, "*Mister!*"

There was something in that shout

that set warning bells ringing inside my head and I twisted around fast, just as Mills, now back on his feet, was closing his right hand around his Colt.

I could no longer afford the luxury of ignoring him. He had just taken that away from me. Now, whether I cared for it or not, I must shoot this man before he shot me.

What happened then was an automatic reflex. My right hand came around, my fingers closed on the edge of my jacket, I flipped it back, out of the way, thanking God that I had not rebuttoned it after having opened it in the restaurant, and then swooped for my .442.

Meanwhile, Mills had cleared leather. His face was contorted by a rage he had no real cause to feel against me. I felt no hatred in return. Why should I? Disgust, perhaps, that he should feel that this was the only way he could improve his standing in the world, but no hatred.

He fired his Colt.

The gun bucked in his hand and amber flame spat from the barrel. I stood my ground, knowing that he had made his shot hastily and that the odds were heavy against it hitting me, and as calmly as I knew how in such circumstances, I brought up my Adams and fired back at him.

The bullet struck Mills in the shoulder and he hunched up beneath its impact and staggered backwards. Over on the other side of the street a woman screamed, and the sound cut right through me. I did not move again, not at once. Momentarily deafened by the gunblasts, I was waiting to see what Mills would do. I hoped he would drop his gun and sink to his knees and then someone could send for a doctor. But somehow I knew it wouldn't be that simple.

Instead he fixed me with that hate-filled glare again, and brought his Colt back up onto me. I yelled, "*Give it up, man!*" but he ignored me, and with no other choice in the matter I shot him again and this time blood spat from out of his shirt and he cried out, corkscrewed around and fell sideways, off the sidewalk.

I knew in that instant that he was dead. That I had killed him.

Somehow everyone else on that bustling street knew it as well, and as I let my gunhand drop back to my side, they began to surge forward to get a closer look at the corpse I had just made. I felt tired beyond my years, suddenly too weak to resist them as they caught me up in their forward tide, and pushed me inexorably along until I found myself standing over the body.

In death Dick Mills looked little better than he had in life. His face had taken on that awful, waxy pallor I knew so well. His eyes looked vaguely dreamy. He looked as if he had died midway through a blink. His mouth was open. His tongue was caught between his teeth, and there was blood on it where he had bitten into it.

I wanted to be sick.

The sky darkened ominously. The street was absolutely silent.

It was then that the storm finally struck. Fat raindrops began to pound the roofs and overhangs and gather into puddles in the street. I watched it slap Dick Mills in the face and dilute his blood so that it blurred like watercolour. Around me the rubber-neckers hurried for cover, but I just stood there and let the wind-driven rain lash me, hoping against hope that it would cleanse me: that it would wash away my guilt, the killing curse that Fate had bestowed upon me.

But it didn't.

It didn't.

3

THE old-timers had a phrase for it. *Bite or get bit*. And, as far as it went, that was exactly how it was, that business with Dick Mills. But knowing that, and understanding it, did little to expunge the guilt I felt at taking the fellow's life. Try as I might, I could not escape the shameful waste of it. It was all so pointless.

At the end of the day, a man's life — *and* death — should *mean* something. But what had Mills' life meant? What great, divine purpose had there been in bringing him into the world, of watching him grow and then allowing him to be cut down so young, and for no good reason? As near as I could tell, his life had served no useful purpose, and as for his death, the death I had given him . . .

I stood there in the rain, looking

down at his corpse, for a long time before the storm passed over and a sheriff's deputy finally appeared on the scene. Coming to stand beside me, he looked down at the dead man and nodded sagely.

"Ah," he pronounced almost at once. "Dick Mills."

I glanced at him. My voice was a croak. "You knew him?"

"I did," replied the deputy. "And a hellion he was that one." He shook his head and his tongue made a clicking sound against the roof of his mouth. "What happened?"

I told him. He asked me who I was and when I told him that as well, he gave me that sidelong glance I had come to hate. Yes, I thought sourly. *The* Ash Colter.

Rapidly now I was learning to hate the name, because the Ash Colter these people thought they knew was something of a celebrity, just like his former partner, whereas all *I* wanted was peace and privacy, simply to be left alone.

The deputy took some more details from me and then a couple of witnesses offered their version of events. Very soon it became obvious to him that I had acted only in self-defence, and after much provocation. Eventually he told me that I was free to go, but that I must not attempt to leave town until the coroner's court could confirm a verdict of lawful killing.

I left that quarter of town and followed the weathered boardwalks until at last they led me back to my hotel. The clerk was nowhere to be found, which was a very good thing for him, so I helped myself to my key and went up to my room and shut the rest of the world out.

I knew that the sense of guilt that was overwhelming me was irrational. Dick Mills had given me no choice in the matter. He might just as well have put his own gun to his temple and committed suicide. It was, as the old-timers rightly said, *Bite or get bit.*

But the shooting of Dick Mills

was only secondary to my now all-consuming disquiet, for whilst I had thought it possible to renounce the gun and lead a more peaceful life, whilst I had deluded myself thinking that I could leave all that behind me just by severing my relationship with the man who had taught me the art of killing and riding a couple of hundred miles from the violence of Yellow Creek, Fate had now shown me that it was not going to be as easy as I had hoped.

I cannot remember much about the days that followed the incident with Dick Mills, save that I put myself through a very special kind of hell over the next sixty-odd hours. I paid a girl to fetch my meals and ate in my room. But I ate very little. My sleep was bitty and tortured. I sat there on my bed and looked at the .442 in the holster on the dressing-table and I cursed the weapon, as if it were solely to blame for all that had gone wrong in my life.

The sun disappeared beyond the horizon and the room was plunged into darkness. Still I sat there, unmoving. My mind was fogged with images of Dick Mills, hunching up beneath the hammer of my bullets, twisting around in some gruesome balletic display, falling to earth with his lifeless limbs flapping and, finally, staring up at the sky with eyes frozen midway through a blink, while the rain needled his waxy face and watered down his spilled blood.

A very special kind of hell, yes.

And then, three days later, there came a brisk rap at the door that drew me from my trance. I rose, crossed the room, unlocked the door and opened it, just a crack.

I did not immediately recognise the man who was standing there. Then I had it. He was the clerk I had spoken to at the offices of the Cattlemen's Association the day of the shooting.

He gave me a rather queer look, and suddenly I realised that I must look like hell. Certainly I felt that way. Self-consciously I reached up and touched my jaw. Three days' growth of whiskers rasped against the pads of my fingers. The clerk said uncertainly, "I'm sorry to, uh, disturb you, Mr Colter . . . "

I shook my head and gestured that he should not concern himself on my account.

"Mr Black has instructed me to ask if you would meet him out at the stockyards at two o'clock this afternoon. If you can, uh, make it."

Mr Black. In my blinkered intemperance I had all but forgotten about him. I had to clear my throat before I could speak because I had said very little in the previous few days, and I had grown used to the silence.

"Thank you. You . . . you may tell Mr Black that I shall be there."

I closed the door on him, heard him turn and walk away upon creaking boards. For the first time I became aware that a stranger was in the room with me. I saw him in the reflection of the dressing-table mirror as I turned away from the door, and he made me halt and study him closer.

I looked a mess. My hair was ruffled and matted, my eyes were dark-ringed and hollow, I was in need of a shave and my clothes were creased and rumpled. I ran the fingers of one hand up through my hair. I had been a fool to let myself go to such an extent. By his own stupidity, Dick Mills really *had* killed himself. I would be foolish indeed if I forfeited my life because of his folly.

I took my watch from my vest pocket and opened it. It was a little after eleven o'clock in the morning. I had three hours to put myself to rights.

I had grown used to inactivity and my limbs felt heavy and stiff. But I knew a good cure for that. I picked up my hat and put it on. I paused briefly then, and stared at my gun for a long moment before I finally decided to wear it. In truth, I had carried it for so many years that I felt strange without it. And whether I loved the thing or hated it, it had saved my life more times than I could count. We were linked by an invisible, unbreakable bond, the gun and I.

The hotel clerk looked at me as if he were seeing me for the first time. And certainly he had never seen such a bedraggled version of Ash Colter before. When I asked him, he seemed almost eager to give me directions to a barbershop.

You will need no word-picture from me as to what followed: a haircut and shave, and a lengthy wallow in tepid bath-water while my suit was sponged and pressed at a local laundry-house. Some time later, once I had dried myself off, I donned my spare shirt and buttoned it to the throat. The crisp white cotton felt clean against my skin. I finished dressing, paid my tab and left the barbershop. If I was not exactly a new man, I was at least an improved version of the old one.

I found an eaterie and ordered a meal. Only when it arrived did I realise that I hadn't really eaten anything since just before my encounter with Dick

Mills. But I thrust him from my mind. What had I thought when first he had braced me? That he was an accident waiting to happen. Well, I could see now that indeed he was. And, more importantly, that his particular brand of accident could have happened to anyone. It just so happened to be me.

At about one-thirty I prepared my mustang for riding, swung up into my saddle and headed west, bound for the stockyards at which I had been told to meet Mr Black. The day was bright and the wind was brisk, but the coming winter seemed to have temporarily given way to milder conditions.

The stockyards had spread out alongside the curve of the railroad tracks about a mile and a half outside of town, and occupied some fifty acres of land. As I approached them, I saw an apparently endless tapestry of brown and brindle-coloured cattle, each bunch separated into just-about-manageable lots of twenty five or thirty by means of orderly pole corrals.

As I rode closer, I saw that the yards were a riot of activity, for a train was squatting on the tracks beside the pens, exhaling steam almost impatiently, as if anxious to be on its way. Men were whistling and yelling as they used prods to force unwilling, bawling animals up wooden chutes and into the long line of slat-sided cars. It was a hard job, that one, and every cowboy I had ever met thoroughly detested it, but it had to be done and so they grabbed their prods and went at it with the same rough kind of enthusiasm they displayed for just about everything else in life.

I swung my horse around in a wide sweep, wondering how I was going to find the man whose wire had brought me here. Eventually I reined down before a knot of coffee-drinking, tired-looking rangemen and asked them to point me in Black's direction.

One of them, a beefy fellow in flapping, unbuckled chaps, gestured towards the north and said, "Black?

You'll find Black an' his cronies top end of the stockyards. Can't miss 'em. They're th'only ones around heah ain't dressed fer work. Aside from you, a'course."

We grinned at each other, just to show that no offence had been offered or taken, and then I rode on. Some distance away, and well out of reach of the yellow dust that rose and drifted around the busy yards, I saw a stalled buck wagon and, beside it, a large, olive-coloured tent. It was an incongruous sight, quite the last thing I had been expecting to see, and I assumed that this was where I would find the man I was after.

I rode closer. A man in a long, off-white duster and some sort of peaked cap was idling beside the ornate wagon, and I aimed my mustang towards him. When he saw me coming he pushed away from the vehicle and came forward to meet me. Wind sent little waves through the material of the tent and made the loose-hanging flap pop and crackle.

"He'p you?" he asked, looking up at me with his head cocked to one side and his eyes narrowed against the unseasonal sunlight.

As I made to reply, the tent-flap was suddenly pushed aside and a portly man in a spotless brown suit came outside, having no doubt heard the sounds of my arrival.

I studied him. He had a corpulent, pasty face and very dark eyes that seemed to view the world from out of liquefied pouches. He was about fifty years of age, and his hair was so completely black that I could only conclude that he coloured it artificially. It grew thick at the sides, I noticed, but he had to scrape what little remained on top artfully across a pink pate. He had long sideburns, as was the fashion of the day, and a black, pencil-line moustache.

He laboured over to us, a careful smile playing at his mouth as he ranged his eyes across me. I felt ill at ease with his scrutiny, for it was more as if he were judging a prize bull than a man.

"Mr Colter?" he asked as he finally came to stand before my horse.

I answered him with a similar question. "Mr Black?"

His face broke into a genial smile and he nodded forcefully. "My dear sir," he said, breathing hard. "Step down and come meet the others! Tapper, take care of the gentleman's horse, if you please! This way, Mr Colter!"

I dismounted, passed my reins to the fellow in the duster, allowed the affable Simon Black to pump my hand effusively and then followed on as he led me towards the tent.

"Quite dreadful, that spot of bother you ran into the other day," he said over his shoulder. "I felt quite ill when the editor of the *Advocate* came up to tell me. I'm sure I don't know what Fort Wray is coming to, Mr Colter. Still, thank goodness the fellow didn't harm you."

He stopped suddenly and I almost walked into him. He turned around and studied me critically. "He *didn't* harm you . . . did he?" he asked quietly.

"If you mean Mills," I said, "no, he didn't."

Black looked relieved. "Well, that's a mercy, for I'm afraid that what we are proposing is certainly no job for a convalescent."

We continued on towards the tent. There was something theatrical in the way he brushed back the flap and bade me enter before him. He was something of a performer, I judged, and he was trying to make my entrance a thing of drama for the benefit of his companions.

His companions.

I ducked my head and went inside. Immediately I was struck by the way the material of the tent turned the filtering sunshine into a weird green twilight. I came to another halt and surveyed the scene before me.

A portable table had been erected in

the centre of the flimsy structure, and behind it sat four men, on collapsible chairs of hardwood and canvas. A silver ice bucket sat in the middle of the table, and projecting from it I saw the long, green-glass neck of a champagne bottle. Beside this was a humidor, the lid of which had been left up to expose a line of fat, expensive Cuban cigars. Each man had a glass on the table before him, with bubbles popping sluggishly to the surface of what little champagne remained in them.

Mr Black dropped the flap behind him and with a flourish, introduced me to the others. Arthur Shaw. A G Tyrell. Sam Reasoner. John Chase. As I nodded to each one in turn, it was not difficult to see that they were cattle-barons, once-tough men who had carved empires out of this rough land and now spent their declining years growing rich and turning soft.

They were all dressed in a curious combination of big city finery and old reminders of their former glory.

They complemented their expensive grey suits with battered Stetsons and scuffed, spur-hung boots. They quaffed champagne because they felt that they should, but I knew that any one of them would gladly have emptied his glass into the thirsty earth if it meant he could then refill it with raw, snakehead whisky.

They, like Black, weighed me up with shrewd eyes but said very little, other than to mutter a perfunctory greeting. After that, Mr Black gestured for me to take the single chair on the near side of the table and, as he laboured around to retake his own chair among the cattlemen, he offered me a drink, which I declined.

Once he was installed in his creaking seat, Black put his elbows on the table, steepled his fingers and said, "I'm sure I don't need to remind you that whatever we say here this afternoon is to be treated in the strictest confidence . . . "

"Of course."

"Then I'll come right to the point, Mr Colter. We — that is, these gentlemen and some other members of the Cattlemen's Association — have been experiencing some trouble with the outlaw John Kidd. You've heard of Kidd, I take it?"

I nodded. Everyone had heard of Kidd, even back then. "Rustling?" I prompted.

Black said, "That is one word for it. Kidd has organised some sort of bully-boy racket in our neck of the woods. If one of our members 'donates' a certain number of cattle to Kidd and his men, they in turn guarantee to 'protect' the ranch from rustlers." He snorted his disgust. "The nerve of the man!" he said, and his cronies shuffled around and muttered their agreement. "If they refuse, Kidd goes ahead and helps himself anyway."

"And you want this business stopped."

"Indeed we do."

"Where has he been operating, Mr Black?"

"Mostly to the south and east of here, down along the Arikaree. As near as we can figure it, he hides the stolen stock away somewhere near the Kansas line, blots their brands and then pushes them east, over the line and thence on to a buyer down towards the Smoky Hills country. By the time he's reached his destination and is ready to sell them, the doctored brands have healed nicely. Any but the most experienced cattleman would think they'd been there for years."

I thought about it. I thought, *John Kidd*. Now there *was* a challenge! Eventually I said, "That would explain why you're offering such a high salary. Kidd is quite the man of the moment."

It was no lie. If all was to be believed, he had a wild and reckless nature that had captured the public's imagination. He had been born in '54 and spent his childhood years learning all forms of rascality — and pistolmanship — at his grandfather's knee. The rustling of horses and cattle was evidently a kind of tradition within the Kidd family. But John had gone one step further. He had branched out into the road-agenting game, starting with stage hold-ups and graduating to trains and finally banks. It was, by all accounts, quite a lucrative trade. Rumour had it that he had taken twenty thousand dollars from a bank in Denver the previous April just by threatening to blow the place up with some liquid he had claimed to be what we now call nitroglycerin.

"We are realists, Mr Colter," said Black, curtailing my thoughts. "We are as aware of John Kidd's reputation as are you. We know we need to hire the best man for the job. And the best man invariably comes expensive."

I considered it some more, knowing that they were expecting a response right here and now. I could use the money, there was no denying that. And there was no way I could hope to earn a comparable sum within such a relatively short space of time anywhere else. I did not know the terrain, it was true, but I could hire someone for that. And I was a fast learner.

At last I nodded. "Very well, gentlemen," I said. "I'm game for it. I can't give you a definite time limit, of course, but you have my word that I'll find this fellow and chase him clean across the border for you."

That sent another little ripple through them. They shifted around and threw meaningful looks at each other, and Mr Black shuffled his high-button boots under the table and gave me an unctuous smile. "I fear you may have misunderstood our meaning, Mr Colter," he said. "We are paying you to *kill* this man, not just chase him away."

Something cold made itself known in the pit of my stomach, and I knew that what had brought it to life was the word *kill*. I looked at them. Outside, by the pens, a man yelled something at an ornery cow and the cow bawled indignantly back at him. Some of the condensation beading the neck of the champagne bottle suddenly trickled down into the ice bucket.

I said, "I fear we have both made a mistake, Mr Black. I am not an assassin. I do not kill men for money. I would prefer not to kill another man ever again."

"We want Kidd dead," said the grizzled old man Black had called Arthur Shaw. He looked as if he had shrunk down inside a suit that was a size too big for him, and when he spoke, one of those fat Cuban cigars danced at the edge of his mouth. "After all the trouble he's been to us, nothing less will do."

I stood up. "Then perhaps you had better find yourselves another man," I suggested formally. "I'm sorry if you feel I have wasted your time, gentlemen."

Black, also standing up, said, "Hold on a moment, Colter. Can't we at least discuss this?"

"That depends on how much you want this Kidd out of your hair," I replied. "Now, I will catch him and bring him to justice, or I will run him out of the territory for good and all. But I will not kill him if I can possibly help it."

"We want him dead," said Sam Reasoner. "On that we are agreed, Mr Colter."

"Then I wish you luck in finding a man for the task," I said with a nod. "Good day, gentlemen."

I turned and pushed out into the fresher air of the brisk afternoon, with its din of men and animals and the shrill, high whistle of the huffing train, and went across to the buck wagon to untie my horse. I nodded farewell to the man in the duster, Tapper, and led the animal around and put one foot in the stirrup. By that time Simon Black had followed me outside, and stood watching as I settled myself more comfortably in my saddle.

"Please, Mr Colter," he said, squinting up at me from out of his curiously liquefied eyes. "Don't let's be so hasty here. I'm sure we can come to some more equitable agreement. Perhaps if we were to offer you more money . . . ?"

I shook my head. "I'm sorry, Mr Black," I replied. "I've killed enough men in my time. I'll kill no more, if I can help it. And no amount of money will make me change my mind on that."

He looked up at me and saw that I would not be swayed. His shoulders dropped and he nodded in resignation. "Very well. I thank you for coming, sir. and . . . and I wish you well in the future."

"And I you," I said, and rode away from him until, at last, the drifting, yellow dust obscured me from his sight.

4

PRINCIPLES are fine and noble things, of course, and I knew I should have felt quite proud of myself as I headed back to Fort Wray. But I could not help regretting the loss of such a munificent salary, for I had been counting on the money to give me a new start in life. Still, there was little to be done about it now. I would just have to begin a fresh search for some other source of employment.

As I rode back to town, the early winter darkness was already leeching the colour from the sky, and it was turning distinctly chilly again. I slowed the mustang to a walk as I entered the town limits, my immediate impulse being to return to my hotel and consider my position. But I had already spent enough time within those four walls, and suddenly I felt an uncharacteristic urge to have a drink or two instead. Tomorrow was soon enough to begin the process of picking up and organising the threads of my life. For now, I might as well lose myself in a merry crowd.

I pointed my horse up the street, not knowing where I would end up. Street-flares had already been lit along most of the main arteries, and I headed for the place that offered the most light, that lively part of the town where I had been braced by Dick Mills.

I reached a saloon calling itself The Mother Lode, dismounted and tied my horse to the rack out front. At that time of the afternoon the place was still relatively quiet, which suited both my mood and my purpose. I walked up to the far end of the bar and ordered a beer. It came and I stood there with one foot on the brass rail, alone with my thoughts.

The saloon was pleasantly warm. A wagon-wheel chandelier cast cones of dim saffron light down over the other customers. Some, like me, stood up at the bar, while the rest were seated at the round, scratched tables that took up the centre of the big, sawdusted room. In one corner, a man in a striped shirt and a derby hat broke the low babble of conversation by playing odd snatches of tunes on an old piano. A few girls moved among the patrons, trying to entice them to spend their money on high-priced, so-called 'effervescent wine', but I was too introspective and remote to pay them much heed, and so they left me alone.

I thought about the proposition that had been put to me earlier on. Had I known what was expected of me, I probably would never have come to Fort Wray. And if I had not come here, Dick Mills would doubtless still be alive, and I would not have his death adding weight to all the others I still carried with me.

The beer was flat and tasteless. I pushed the schooner away from me and when the bartender came over with a question in his expression, I ordered a whiskey. That was more to my taste, and I took it to a quiet corner table and spent the next twenty minutes just savouring it.

At last full dark filled up the oilpaper windows and a few more customers drifted in and named their poison. I drained my glass and made to rise and leave.

It was then that I heard someone snap his fingers, and when I turned my head and glanced up, I found a man looking down at me and muttering, "Now, don't tell me . . . It's Colter, isn't it? The famous Ash Colter?"

I peered at him closer. "You have me at a disadvantage," I said. I remember that my words slurred a little, for I was not really much of a drinker, and even a modest amount of alcohol swiftly worked its disorientating effect upon me.

The fellow looked quite pleased with himself. "Well, I'll *be*!" he murmured. "Fancy me running into one of the country's most illustrious sons. May I buy you another drink, Mr Colter? I'd consider it an honour."

I knew I had had enough, but by that time I was just sufficiently drunk to throw caution to the wind, and so I said that indeed he might. He turned at the waist and, raising one hand, snapped his fingers to get the bartender's attention. "A bottle of your finest over here, if you please!"

He was tall and sturdily put-together, quite young-looking, with a well-defined jaw, slightly insolent blue eyes and a generous nose. His suit marked him as some sort of an office worker. He took a seat across from me and, a moment later, the bartender brought over a bottle of Old Kentucky and a spare glass. My new-found companion poured himself a drink and a refill for me, then raised his glass and said, "Your good health, Mr Colter!"

We clinked our glasses together and I sipped some more.

"My goodness, but I've followed your exploits for quite a few years now," he enthused. "The Snake River Shootout . . . that dreadful business down on the Washita with Custer . . . the hell-towns of Elton and Yellow Creek . . . You have lived a full life, sir, and no mistake!"

I shrugged, unwilling to discuss those old times. I set my glass down, realising at last that I had drunk more than was wise for me, and again prepared to leave.

My companion frowned. "You're not going?" he asked with some disappointment. "My dear sir, see it from my point of view. This is the kind of opportunity that only comes once in a man's life, to talk with a legend!"

"My apologies," I replied carefully. "I thank you for the drink, and wish you well."

I had just started to rise when he said, "But we have so much to discuss! Your friend Page, for instance. And what of this business with John Kidd?"

I sat down again and frowned at him. So far as I knew, my business with the Cattlemen's Association had been confidential. Simon Black himself had affirmed the desire for secrecy before we had embarked upon our discussion. It occurred to me then that this had been no chance encounter. This man was a reporter, in search of a story. I was a fool not to have realised it sooner, for did the Cattlemen's Association not have its offices above the Fort Wray *Advocate*?

"I have no comment to make on the matter," I said stiffly.

But he was a tenacious fellow, and he was set on pursuing it. "For what it's worth," he said, "I think you did a wise thing in declining the Association's offer."

The drink had turned me surly. "And what would *you* know about it?"

He shrugged. "Like all well-informed men, I know of Kidd's reputation. Any man would be wise to steer clear of him."

"I did not make my decision out of cowardice, sir."

"And neither am I saying that you did, Mr Colter," he replied easily. "But all the same, you have an enviable reputation of your own to consider. You must be reluctant to take even the slightest chance that Kidd might shatter it."

The fellow really was infuriating. "And who says that he would?" I barked.

"Why, the outcome of any such encounter is a foregone conclusion, surely. Kidd has a brilliant intellect, and they say he is unchained lightning with a gun. Any man who set himself up to capture or kill such a fellow would have his work cut out for him."

I waved one hand dismissively. "You know little of the matter, sir."

"Well, you can't blame a fellow for being curious, Mr Colter. The Cattlemen's Association of Colorado offers you a quite staggering sum to track down one man, and you *refuse* it? What is the public supposed to think, if not that you are reluctant to face the legendary Kidd?"

"I have my reasons," I gritted.

My tormentor shrugged vaguely and dug into his pocket. "Very well," said he. "Have it your own way. But I can promise you this, and I trust you will take no offence, for I mean it well — once word gets around, people are going to ask themselves if Ash Colter is all he's cracked up to be." He withdrew something from his pocket and tossed it into the centre of the table. "For the drinks," he said, and got up, turned around and strode out of the saloon.

I watched him go, feeling indignant and yet knowing I was a fool to feel that way. I had my reasons, as I had told him, and good reasons they were, too.

I got to my feet and was just about to leave when I thought to glance down and see what he had tossed so carelessly onto the table. Although it had been screwed into a ragged ball, I could see that it was a bill of some kind. But it was not a bill with which I was at all familiar.

Slowly I reached down, picked it up and opened it out.

The breath caught sharply in my throat — for it was a ten thousand dollar note!

It is true that my mind had been dulled by liquor, but not so much that I could not immediately grasp the significance of my find. According to the reports I had read at the time, John Kidd had been given just such a note in with the money he had taken from the Denver bank robbery the previous April. Since he could not hope to change it anywhere without drawing unwelcome attention to himself, it was assumed that he had either kept it as a memento, that he had traded it among his own kind for something of more use to him, or that he had thrown it away.

If this were that note, as seemed likely, then . . .

I stared at the bill, my thoughts thrown into a veritable maelstrom.

. . . *then the fellow who had just been goading me must have been John Kidd himself!*

The realisation of it struck me like a slap in the face, and worked a sobering effect upon me. Abruptly I stuffed the bill into my pocket and left the saloon at a run, drawing all eyes to me. I slammed out through the batwing doors, nearly collided with two big miners on the boardwalk, leapt down into the dirt and scanned the street for sign of the outlaw.

I could see him nowhere.

A curse hissed out beneath my breath, and I was startled to find that my fists were bunched. *The nerve of the fellow!* I thought, breathing hard. But now that I considered it, I could see that it would be just like Kidd to risk his very liberty in order to play such a prank, for I have already mentioned his somewhat reckless nature, and the way in which such foolhardy actions had endeared him to the public at large.

But with that thought came another. Had our encounter been merely a prank? Or was it more in the way of a challenge? I turned slowly and went back into the saloon to settle my tab. Perhaps there was some truth in what he had said. It was only to be expected that the public would misconstrue my refusal to track him down as an act of cowardice. And once they heard about tonight's little episode, as Kidd himself would make sure they did, I would become a laughing stock.

I could not allow that to happen.

I slapped some coins down on the bar, too preoccupied to pay much attention to the looks I was getting from The Mother Lode's other patrons. Outside, I mounted my horse and rode directly to Simon Black's office. My mind was made up, and even though I was allowing my pride to over-rule my good common sense, I knew I could not walk away from Kidd's challenge, not if I wanted to retain my good name.

It was fortunate for me that Black was a diligent man and that he had decided to work late, otherwise I would have had to wait until morning. As it was, he appeared understandably surprised when I burst in upon him less than a quarter of an hour later and requested five minutes of his time. Graciously, however, and with some curiosity, I think, he bade me enter and closed the door behind him.

"If your offer's still open, Mr Black," I said, "I'd like to take you up on it."

He frowned at me in the low, cosy light of the lamp on his big desk. "My dear sir . . . Whatever has happened to change your mind?"

I shook my head. "Nothing. A personal matter. Is the offer still open?"

"Why, of course. But . . . but what about that rather fundamental disagreement between us?"

"I haven't changed my mind about that," I told him. "I'll not kill another man if I can help it. But you have my word on this much — if it's at all possible, I'll bring John Kidd in to stand trial for his crimes. That way, when the court gets through with him, you and your Association members should be able to watch him hang." I looked him over carefully. "Do you think they'd be satisfied with that?"

He pondered it, and gradually what began as a slight inclination of the head turned into another of his emphatic nods. "Yes, Mr Colter. I think I might be able to talk them around to that."

I extended my right hand. "Then we have a deal?" I asked neutrally.

He took my hand and we shook. "We have a deal, Mr Colter," he said enthusiastically. "Damned if we don't!"

★ ★ ★

The next few days were taken up with organisation, for it was just not possible to embark upon such a manhunt as this promised to be with any degree of speed. If we were to stand any chance of success, I must plan it like a military campaign, with little or nothing left to providence. And, just like a military campaign, I would have need of troops.

I knew better than to raise a small army, of course. To catch Kidd we would need to be light and manoeuvrable. So I asked Simon Black to find me the five best men he could, and about four days later they arrived in Fort Wray.

When I got my first good look at them, I was not immediately sure of the men he had chosen. They struck me as a motley collection, and their big-brimmed sombreros and Stetsons, their bright silk bandannas, flapping bullhide chaps and spur-heavy stovepipe boots made them look better suited to rangework than the kind of undertaking I had in mind.

Three of them were in their late twenties or early thirties. According to Black they were all top hands, and he had evidently selected them as much for their abilities with handgun and rifle as for the loyalty they displayed to their respective brands.

Saul Yarbrough was a big, genial black man with a round, shiny face and an easy grin. When I shook hands with him I felt something of his prodigious strength, and when I looked into his eyes they told me that I could rely upon him implicitly. John Horan was sober and unsmiling, with eyes the colour of gunsmoke, while Henry Morse was short and heavy-set, with a long, dark moustache and a tuft of brown beard that projected comically from his squarish chin.

At some fifty years, Lemuel Winch was the oldest of the men. He was a big, powerful man of mixed blood, whose wiry hair was as shaggy and dishwater grey as his full beard. I had never seen a cowboy like him before — or since, for that matter. He favoured a greasy hunting shirt, buckskin leggings and moccasins. He said very little, for it was his habit to chew constantly at a cud of molasses-cured tobacco. He gave absolutely nothing away, but in fairly short order I learned to trust his judgment, for he knew the country over which we would be moving, and at some time deep in his past I sensed that he had also gained some first-hand experience of the outlaw life as well.

Of them all, it was a young fellow named Bob Bancroft who concerned me the most. He was a personable enough man, but there was a certain immaturity about him that made me wonder if he was right for the job. His broad shoulders and lean, horseman's hips made him a veritable wedge of a man, and his narrow, smooth face, well-spaced hazel eyes, straight nose and winning smile must have made him especially popular with the fairer sex. He wore a Peacemaker in a holster tied low around his left leg, and while he seemed agreeable enough, he appeared to feel that all of this was just a circus, an entertainment concocted for his own personal amusement.

How we managed to gather these men together and still maintain absolute secrecy I will never know, but certainly the need for secrecy was never more important than now. John Kidd had been remarkably well-informed at our earlier meeting. Apparently he knew everything there was to know about why I had come to Fort Wray. It could be that he had heard about the gunfight in which I had been involved, of course, and simply put two and two together. But more likely he had sympathizers in town, spying for him.

Well, that was fair enough. I needed as much information as I could get about *my* quarry, too, and following Dick Mills' inquest, Simon Black arranged for me to meet with Max Taylor, the sheriff of Fort Wray. It was from him that I learned something more of Kidd and his gang.

★ ★ ★

At last I had my army and my information. All that remained was to finalise my plan of attack. But to attack at all, I must first locate my enemy.

Simon Black told me that a rancher down along the Arikaree by the name of Ed Buckhalter had been visited by Kidd and his men twice in the past six weeks. On each occasion Buckhalter had refused to 'donate' any of his stock to the outlaws. As a result, he had lost about twenty head of fine Hereford cattle a fortnight earlier, and it was Black's conviction that he was due for another visit from Kidd, who would want to know if he had changed his mind about the deal he had proposed.

I decided there and then that Buckhalter's ranch was as likely a starting-point as any. My army and I would hole up there and await Kidd's visit. And when Kidd finally showed up . . .

We left Fort Wray and rode southeast later that very same day.

After the hurly-burly of town life, the great sweep of the open range was a revivifying tonic. These were the rich, elevated plains of Colorado, you see: level, grass-thick stretches broken here and there by low hills and bluffs, and the odd, distant tree. It was a land given over predominantly to the production of wheat, but cattle thrived there as well, and this is what made it ideal territory for Kidd and his cronies.

We kept going for what remained of the day. Lem Winch rode out ahead and the rest of us followed him in a loose bunch. Soon night began its powdery approach, and about forty miles from town we finally reached Buckhalter's ranch.

In the rising moon- and star-light, the

place was just a clutter of low buildings and pole fences. The bunkhouse was a long, rough-looking structure with a shingled roof and squares of smoky light at the small, high windows, while the main house was a rambling affair surrounded by tie-racks and porch overhangs. We came in at a walk, past an old wagon up on blocks. The barn and other out-buildings were just huge pools of shadow to our left. A dog started yapping at the back of the house. Still out ahead, Winch raised his voice and called, "*Ed!* You in there?"

We brought our horses to a stop before the house, waiting. The early evening was quiet but for the distant bellow of cattle. Then I heard movement within the bunkhouse, men racing quickly across a board floor. At the same moment, the door to the main house swung open and a man's silhouette came out onto the porch, a rifle held waist-high and trained on us.

"Who is it?" the man snapped,

his voice high and feisty. "Identify yourselves."

In that same instant, someone yanked the bunkhouse door open and I heard more rifles being levered.

Our horses fidgeted uneasily. Winch called, "What's a matter, Ed — don't you recognise me?"

The silhouette on the porch was silent for a moment. Then the man — obviously Buckhalter — said, "Lem?"

"Wal, it's a mite early for Santy Claus."

There was relief in Buckhalter's tone now, as he put down his long gun. "All right, boys," he called to the two men who had come out of the bunkhouse. "Put up your guns. It's Lem Winch."

As he came down into the dark yard, a girl appeared in the doorway behind him, carrying a lantern. She followed Buckhalter outside, an oval of buttery lamplight spilling drunkenly around her, and when she and Buckhalter came to a halt before Winch's ragged, ugly-faced pony, she held the lantern high so that he could get a better look at us.

Buckhalter ran his troubled green eyes across us. He was a tall, trim man of about five and forty years, dressed in a heavy flannel shirt and dark pants that were baggy at the knees. Holding his rifle in his left hand, he brought the right up and hooked a thumb into one of his thick suspenders. Then he said, "I thought for a minute you was — "

"Kidd?"

I had spoken before I realised it.

He looked at me and I said, "Has he been here, Mr Buckhalter? Recently?"

He looked at me for some time. At length he said, "And who are you?"

Leaning forward, I handed him down a letter of introduction Simon Black had prepared for me on official Cattlemen's Association notepaper. While Buckhalter unfolded it, held it to the light and squinted at it, I felt the eyes of the girl on me, and glanced back at her.

She did not look away. The light

washed down over the smooth planes of her face and set little lights glowing deep inside eyes as green as those of Buckhalter. She had a small nose that was appealingly snubbed, a wide, full mouth and a strong chin that swept back into the soft line of her throat. Her dark blonde hair spilled down over the shoulders of her thick shirt, and showed gold here and there where the light caught on all the twists and curls.

"My daughter, Ruth," Buckhalter said suddenly, and I realised that he had finished reading the letter and put his eyes back onto me. When I looked down at him, he was offering his hand. "Pleased to meet you, Colter. And to answer your question — no, Kidd ain't shown hide nor hair around here since he lifted some of my cattle two weeks ago. But take my word for it, he's due. I can *feel* it."

I looked over at Lem Winch. His smile revealed long, tobacco-stained teeth.

"Now," said Buckhalter, thawing somewhat. "You fellers light and put up your horses. We got stew on, if you're hungry."

And so began the hardest job of all — just waiting. But as you will see, we did not have to wait long before our man showed up.

5

WE quartered ourselves in the barn, and at my orders the horses were kept ready to ride at a moment's notice.

But for the first three days nothing happened, and soon the waiting began to pall upon my men, who were not used to such inactivity. Bob Bancroft was the one who showed his impatience most of all, but it was Henry Morse who came over to me on the second day and asked if he might go and help Buckhalter's men in their chores.

I shook my head. "Best we stay out of sight as much as we can, Henry," I replied. "If Kidd is as shrewd as I think he is, he'll scout this place thoroughly before he rides in. First sign that something's not right around here and he won't show up."

Henry clearly wasn't happy about it,

but apart from a little muttering, he just turned and walked away.

The men occupied themselves with endless games of poker or cribbage, although Winch kept apart from the rest and just sat cross-legged at the back of the barn, chewing and spitting, chewing and spitting. In the evenings we ate with Buckhalter's waddies. He employed three men, and he also did much of the work around the place himself.

Time passed. I knew that we would be lucky indeed if anything happened right away. But by the dawn of the fourth day, I began to wonder if this was such a likely starting-point after all.

The day before, Winch had come to me with the suggestion that he ride out and scout the surrounding countryside for sign of our quarry. For all we knew, he said, Kidd might have quit this neck of the woods altogether, and we were just sitting around here on a fool's errand.

I considered it. "Trouble is, if Kidd or one of his men spot you, they might guess what we're up to."

He treated me to another of his tobacco-stained smiles. "They *won't* spot me, cap'n," he muttered, and somehow I believed him.

He rode out twenty minutes later, and uncannily he was soon lost to sight, having blended seamlessly with the surrounding country.

I was idling in the barn doorway around the middle of the fourth morning, watching the flat plains extending away to distant blue mountains, when Ruth Buckhalter came over to greet me. I had not had much to do with her following our arrival, but I had seen her around a few times and she had always accorded me an affable nod of greeting. Today she had eschewed her usual practical shirt and canvas pants and instead wore a smart gingham dress that displayed her hourglass figure to good advantage.

"Good morning, Mr Colter," she

said as she came to a halt before me.

Henry Morse and John Horan were exercising our horses in the corral at the rear of the barn. As had become his custom, Saul Yarbrough was reading a book, frowning in concentration as his lips moved in a whisper. Bob Bancroft was sleeping with his hat pulled low over his eyes.

I dipped my head. "Ma'am."

"Daddy asked me to see if you would share supper with us tonight. Your man Bancroft shot a couple of rabbits yesterday afternoon and I'm baking them in a pie."

I'd heard that Bancroft had slipped away to do some foraging, even though he had known it was against my orders to go too far and risk drawing attention to himself. When the time was right I intended to discipline him over it, for he was of no use to me or any of us if he put our plan in jeopardy.

But to the girl I only said, "Thank you, ma'am. I'd be honoured."

"Good. It'll make a pleasant change. We don't see much of you or your men."

"That's the idea, Miss Buckhalter."

"I suppose so. But do you think you might bend the rules just long enough to walk me back to the house?"

I laughed. "The house is barely more than forty yards from here."

She shrugged. "Well . . . we can always take the long way around."

It should be all right, I thought. I had long since changed from my usual suit and string tie into Levis, a workshirt and sheepskin jacket, so from a distance I would pass for just one more hired hand. I said, "All right, then."

I stepped out into the weak sunshine and we began a slow stroll that took us around the ranch-buildings and roughly parallel to the border where the dirt yard met the fine surrounding grassland.

"They say you are a killer, Mr Colter," the girl said, quite unexpectedly. "And yet I must say, you don't strike me as such."

"You have met enough killers to be able to judge?" I asked.

She smiled and shrugged again. "Daddy's men say you killed a man in Fort Wray just last week."

"Daddy's men seem to say a lot."

She eyed me sidelong. "You'd sooner not talk about it," she guessed.

I nodded, and glanced down at her. "Perhaps we can talk about you instead."

"What would you like to know?"

"Anything you would care to tell me."

"Well," she said, considering. "I am twenty three years old. My middle name is Catherine. Since my mother died in childbirth and Daddy never remarried, I have no brothers or sisters. I am a passably good cook, deft with a needle and thread, I can wash and iron and I knit and sing quite well, and one of these days Daddy says I am going to make someone a very good wife."

"Anyone in particular?"

"Not yet. I've still got too much to do here."

"Looking after this place?"

"This place. My father. And he needs someone to look after him, too, otherwise he'd spend his every waking moment just working." Her face clouded and she gestured to our surroundings with a brief sweep of one hand. "Daddy settled this land more than twenty years ago. He fought tooth and nail to hold it when the Utes went on the warpath back in '73. Until Kidd came in six weeks ago, we felt safe here, secure."

"But Kidd changed all that," I hazarded.

She nodded. "Yes. And that upset Daddy more than he's willing to admit."

We had gone in a wide half-circle by this time, and were now walking around behind the house. The day was bright and dry, more like the days they usually have in that part of Colorado, but I still didn't like the look of the dark clouds I could see smothering the peaks of those distant mountains.

"Don't you ever get lonely out here?" I asked, changing the subject.

She glanced away from me, but not before I saw hurt sparking in her green eyes. "I'm the only girl for forty miles around," she said tiredly, as if she were finally giving voice to something she had often thought. "The nearest eligible bachelor lives thirty miles away. I have no friends of my own or any other age. Of course I'm lonely."

"I'm sorry, Miss Buckhalter. I didn't mean to pry."

She waved one hand vaguely, and forced a game smile back on to her face. "Don't apologise. It's not your fault — though I will confess that having you and your men here over the past few days has really brought it home to me, just how few people we see or know in this part of the country. Oh, and by the way. My given name is Ruth."

I nodded and said it again. "Ruth." It had a fine, soft, velvety sound.

I did not have long to savour it, however, for the moment was broken by the urgent drum of hooves that could only signify a horse coming in fast.

Because we had both been half-expecting trouble sooner or later, we hurried back around the main house without another word. Lem Winch was just bringing his pony to a halt in the yard. As he poured himself effortlessly from his saddle with dust rising around him, the rest of the men appeared in the barn doorway, also drawn by the sounds of his dramatic approach.

He turned his knowing eyes upon me, nudged back his hat and said, "They' comin', cap'n. Kidd an' seven others."

I felt a thrill of anticipation wash through me. "Where?"

He hooked a thumb over one shoulder. "'Bout six, eight miles back thataway."

"Did they see you?"

His response was a withering look, so I changed tack.

"Coming fast?"

"Fast enough, I reckon. Be here inside half an hour, easy."

I nodded. "Right. Ruth, get along inside the house and stay out of sight. Where's your father?"

"There's some boggy ground to the south and east of here. Daddy went to see what he could do about fencing it off."

"Henry — go fetch him. Rest of you men, get yourselves under cover."

Before anyone could do anything, however, John Horan fixed me with his curiously smoky grey eyes, a big Remington rifle with a brass telescopic sight in his hands. "You still aimin' to stick with this plan o' yours, Mr Colter?" he asked quietly.

I looked back at him. He, like Winch, was a man of few words. But there were other, more subtle ways to register disapproval or disagreement, and Horan knew them all. A glance, a sigh, the briefest whispered curse or a sorry shake of the head — he had used them all at one time or another to express his low opinion of my plan.

And perhaps he had some justification. It was, after all, almost too simple. The next time Kidd showed up here, Buckhalter was to send him away with another stubborn refusal to co-operate. We would then follow him at a distance, locate the exact whereabouts of his camp and then raid the place the following dawn and capture the entire gang.

Horan had expressed his reservations about the thing right at the start. He was no more bloodthirsty than any other man I had met, but because Kidd was who he was, Horan believed that the best way to deal with him and his men was simply to catch them in a crossfire and shoot them all.

I should have expected no less. Horan was from Arthur Shaw's ranch, the AS Connected, and if his employer wanted Kidd dead, then so did he.

Still, I was adamant. In the first place, I was not prepared to risk any injury or damage to the Buckhalters, Buckhalter's men or his property. In the second place, our job was to *catch* Kidd. The law could, and would, handle what was to follow.

Now I looked back at Horan as the rest of the men stood around us, waiting. I said, "We're sticking with the plan."

Horan spat. "Well, you know what I think about it. I don't mean you no disrespect, Mr Colter, but your plan stinks."

Henry Morse and Saul Yarbrough drew in low, hissing breaths. Bob Bancroft watched me with a lazy smile on his face. Winch said, "I ain't takin' sides, cap'n, but John's speakin' fer all of us. Feller's sneaky as this here Kidd, you don't give him any kinduva chance a-tall."

I was angry that they should choose this moment to go against me, but there was no time to argue about it, not just then, so I responded only briefly. "You men are here to follow orders," I said. "*Follow* 'em."

Horan held my eyes for a moment longer, then turned and stalked away. I felt a twinge of apprehension in my stomach, but whether it was because of him or just that fluttery feeling that always came before a showdown. I wasn't sure.

Suddenly the yard was a hive of activity, as the men disappeared into the barn, Ruth hurried across the yard and into the house, and Henry went in search of Ed Buckhalter. I looked to the south, but could see no sign of approaching riders.

Ten minutes later Buckhalter came galloping back in with Henry, the long face beneath his loose-brimmed black hat tight and serious. "You be all right?" I asked him briefly, as Henry dragged both his own and Buckhalter's mounts into the barn.

Buckhalter just nodded and strode

towards the house.

He had installed an open iron watertank to one side of the house to aid trough-feeding in winter, and it was to this massive, five thousand-gallon container that I now went. In the distance cattle were bawling, and Ruth's dog, no doubt sensing the electricity in the air, was yapping excitedly. I found myself a good vantage point to one side of the rust-pitted tank and sank onto my haunches.

Some birds flapped past overhead. I peered up, identified them as orioles and brown thrashers. Then I put my eyes back on the flats to the south and suddenly my every muscle stiffened, for I could see them now, coming in line abreast; eight men, walking their horses slowly towards us, their every gesture calculated to menace and intimidate.

I watched them come nearer, until finally I could pick out more details.

I recognised Kidd immediately, even though he was no longer wearing the smart grey suit he had favoured that night at The Mother Lode. I recognised the same insolent blue eyes, the largish nose, the thick flaxen spill of his hair beneath a high-crowned, sand-coloured Stetson, and I found myself wondering if he would suspect a trap. I could feel the ten thousand dollar note in my pants' pocket. Kidd must know I would take up his challenge. But would he suspect a trap *here*?

I could only hope that he would not.

Now my eyes moved along the line to take in Kidd's companions, and I recalled all the details Sheriff Taylor had told me back in Fort Wray.

The man directly to Kidd's left was dressed in a black frock coat and striped grey pants. He had a pinched, mournful looking face and wispy fair hair fanning out from under a black shovel hat. This, I thought, would be Preacher Sweet.

Preacher Sweet was the oldest of the bunch, being some ten years Kidd's senior. He was an Arizona man who had worked variously as a farmer, a clerk and a cowboy before finding religion and becoming an itinerant preacher, specialising in fire and brimstone. He used to burst into crowded saloons and shoot them up in his efforts to make the wayward see the error of their ways, and it was in this fashion that he accidentally shot his first man in 1868. To his surprise he found that he liked the power his big .44-calibre Smith and Wesson Russian gave him, and he had been killing ever since.

The next man was huskier, in his mid-twenties, dressed more like a cowboy. Unless I was mistaken, this was Arnie Bakke, also known as Dutch Arnie. Bakke had started off as a horsebreaker and ranch foreman down in the Edwards Plateau country of southern Texas. Then one day his employer, Frank Chilton, came home early and found him in the not-unwelcoming arms of *Mrs* Chilton. All hell broke loose, and when the gunsmoke cleared, Dutch Arnie was wanted for murder. He, like the Preacher, had been running and killing ever since.

Killin' Jim Middleton came next. He was tall and underfed, whiskery, vague-eyed, with gap-teeth and a wet nose. His unsettled childhood was clearly to blame for the vagaries he displayed as an adult. His mother had been a prostitute and he had known only a string of unsympathetic 'uncles' almost from the time he had first learned to walk. Not surprisingly then, he had grown up into a wild and homicidal twenty four year-old. He was an accomplished horsethief, and rumour had it that he had carried out a number of successful political assassinations down in Mexico.

All of these men I recognised from Sheriff Taylor's descriptions, these and four others — the Mexican gunman Tiburcio Mendez; Buckshot Dave Ryan, the so-called Butcher of Belleville; Al Tate, the Nevada lawman turned outlaw; and Kansas Bill Johnson.

I felt cold in the pit of my stomach.

Unhurriedly they walked their horses into the yard. I saw their heads turning this way and that, scouring every building and patch of cover, naturally suspicious. Then the door to the main house gave a squeak and my eyes swivelled that way just as Buckhalter came out on to his porch with his rifle in his hands.

"That's far enough!" he shouted, and Kidd dutifully reined down and his men followed suit.

All at once the clinking of bits and the creaking of latigo strings died away and the yard was suddenly deafeningly quiet.

I focused my attention on John Kidd. It was hard to credit that he was the man who had so captured the country's imagination. He seemed too ordinary, just one more face in the crowd. There was nothing about him that elevated him above any of the others. His clothes were standard range-wear, his sidearm a common enough Colt .45, his holster plain and functional. He did not even wear it tied down in the manner of gunslingers.

At last he raised his voice. "Now, that's no way to greet old friends," he chided.

Buckhalter snorted disdainfully. He had courage, I thought, to face down all eight of them. "Friends! Rustlers, more like! By Christ, you got a nerve, showing your face around here again, Kidd!"

Kidd's smile was an easy flash of ivory. I looked at him and felt that he didn't give a damn about anyone or anything. He opened his mouth to make some sort of response, but at that moment a long gun suddenly roared out, and Kidd's horse staggered sideways as a big, meaty red hole punched into its neck.

It took us all by surprise. For one vital moment I didn't even understand properly what had happened. I caught a brief glimpse of Kidd's face, the whites of his startled eyes, the edges of his broad mouth yanked down into a grimace as his screaming horse fell sideways. All at once pandemonium reigned in the yard, as Kidd's swearing men fought down their startled horses and tore their handguns from leather.

Kidd kicked free of his stirrups no more than a second or two before his horse hit the dirt with stiff legs and scared eyes. He rolled and was momentarily lost beneath a low cloud of dust. Another shot tore out and the man I had tentatively identified as Kansas Bill Johnson screamed and fell headlong from his saddle.

It came to me then, what had happened, and my teeth clamped together and I came up out of my crouch with my .442 in my hand. *Horan!* I thought. *Horan, damn him!*

By this time Kidd's men had started shooting back, but because they didn't know just who it was they were supposed to be aiming at, their gunfire was wild and indiscriminate. I heard bullets striking wood with a *thap* and a *whop*, bouncing off the watertank with a hornet's whine. From the edge of my vision I saw Ed Buckhalter pivot and fall off the porch. *If anything happened to him or Ruth . . .*

I brought the .442 up, knowing that because of Horan's stupidity we had no choice now but to make a fight of it, and I fired into the insane kaleidoscope of cursing men and turning animals.

Kidd came back up onto his feet, his clothes powdered with the dust of the yard. Al Tate reached down and grabbed one of his upraised arms. He pulled hard and Kidd flung himself up into the saddle behind him. I fired at the two of them, trying to wound, not kill, but in all the confusion my shot went wild.

Then they were out of there, peeling away from the yard in a strung-out, disorganised line, leaving one dying horse and two wounded men in their wake.

I shoved out from behind the watertank. At roughly the same moment Ruth tore open the front door, screamed, "*Daddy!*" and threw herself down into the dirt to cradle her father's head.

As the rest of the men came boiling out of the barn, yelling in their excitement, I crossed swiftly to the downed outlaw, Johnson. He was wriggling about on his back, and blood was making the material of his duck pants stick to the flesh around his left hip.

I looked down at him, my breathing coming fast and my heart racing madly. His face was screwed up into a million creases. His handgun had fallen not far away. It was a big Dragoon. I kicked it well out of his reach before turning my attention to Buckhalter.

He was sitting up now, making little choking sounds as he struggled to handle the pain of his wounded left shoulder. Ruth looked up at me. Her face was a bloodless oval, and tears shone in her big green eyes. Then she turned her attention back to her father and, hearing footsteps behind me, I spun around.

John Horan was in the forefront of the men. Smoke curled from the barrel of his Remington rifle in a string of interlaced question marks. I looked at him. He had deliberately gone against me, and in such a way as to ruin whatever chance of success my plan might otherwise have had.

I stuffed my gun away, crossed the distance between us, reached out, yanked the rifle from his grasp and tossed it away. I saw surprise on his face. He thought he had come to know me over the past few days. He didn't think I could be angry, or show that anger, and he was probably banking on getting clean away with what he had done. But he was about to discover that he didn't know me at all.

It was neither the time nor the place for it, I realised that afterwards, but right then, with gunfire still ringing in my ears —

I swung a roundhouse right that caught him full on the point of the jaw and threw him backwards. The men cleared a path behind him and he went down into the dust. He said, "Damn you, Colter — " and then he went for the Army .44 on his hip, but suddenly Bob Bancroft's gun appeared in his left hand and the ratchety sound it made coming to full cock froze him in his tracks.

"Don't make it two mistakes in the one day, John," he advised quietly.

Horan glared up at him, bleeding from a split lip. Bancroft waited a moment, until he was sure that Horan knew he meant what he'd said, and then he turned the gun away from him and fired it, once. We all flinched as he put the wounded horse out of its misery.

I stabbed a finger down at Horan. "Best you clear out of here now, Horan," I snapped. "You're through on this crew."

"But I — "

I pushed forward, dragging him back up onto his feet and threw him away from me, in the direction of the barn. "Get your horse and get the hell out of here!"

I wanted to say more. I wanted to ask him if it was his boss who had paid him extra to kill Kidd, or all the other big Association cattlemen together. Was that what his fancy rifle and sight was for? But time was wasting. To the others I said, "Get your horses, men. No, not you, Bob. You'd better stay behind and keep an eye on this Johnson."

Although he wasn't happy about it, he nodded acceptance without complaint, and put his sidearm away. Meanwhile, Lem Winch's dark eyes were suddenly lighting up. "We goin' after 'em, cap'n?"

I nodded, and as one the rest of us headed into the stable and caught up our already-saddled mounts. A moment later we thundered out of the yard, heading across the cattle-dotted flats to the south, following the course Kidd and his men had charted not five minutes before. I did not know what we would do when we caught them. I did not even know if we *would* catch them. But I knew that we must at least make some attempt to get the man we were after, for we would never get another chance, not after this.

We pushed our horses up from a canter to a gallop. I narrowed my eyes as the cool wind pushed against my face. I thought about Horan. In spite of his obvious misgivings, I would have put money on him following orders. And yet I had been wrong. And then there was Bancroft. Of all the men, he was the last one I would have expected to come to my defence. And yet I had been wrong about him, too.

We saw Kansas Bill's horse cropping grass away to our left. The animal had instinctively followed the others when they had quit the yard, but it must have stumbled on its trailing reins so often that in the end it just gave up and slowed to a halt.

It lifted its head and watched us thunder past, but made no attempt to join us. A minute or so later, Winch heeled his pony up alongside me. He was pointing at something up ahead. I followed the line of his finger and saw a knot of riders not more than a mile away — Kidd's bunch for sure. I drew my handgun and let my mustang have its head, and the others matched my action and speed.

Someone out ahead must have looked back and seen us coming, for suddenly there came a wink of flame, a puff of smoke, and finally the crack of a gunshot. Winch put his pony on a course that took him away from me, and the rest of the men followed his example so that we now rode fanned out in a line, racing doggedly on after our quarry.

The land beneath us started to rise. We lost Kidd and his men beyond a grassy knoll. When we topped out, I saw a line of trees no more than a quarter of a mile ahead, with a body of water sparkling and winking beyond and between the boughs and boles of firs, aspen and spruce that could only be the Arikaree.

The trees seemed to swallow the outlaws, and instinctively I raised my gunarm to slow the pace. Now that they had cover, they would be infinitely more dangerous than before. And sure enough, within a very short space of time there came the deep, deadly boom of a long gun that made disturbed birds rise up from the timber in a fluttering, squawking mist.

At least one of them had dismounted in the bosque, with the intent to provide some sort of rearguard action for his companions.

Like an officer in the cavalry, I indicated that my men should swing to the left, where a slight rise would give us some cover behind which to consider our next move. But time was not on our side — the longer we were forced to delay, the more distance Kidd and his men would put between us.

We sat our heaving horses for a moment. Then, just as I opened my mouth to start issuing orders, Winch said, "You'uns stay right here, cap'n. I'll signal you when I'm through."

He left his saddle as effortlessly as before and tugged a New Model Sharps carbine from its boot.

"What're you plannin', Lem?" asked Henry Morse.

His response was a broad grin that made his whiskery cheeks rise up and crowd his eyes down to slits. "To blow yonder bushwhacker loose from his drawers," he replied with some glee.

I said, "Lem — " But it was too late — he was already gone.

This time I tried to watch him go, but again the land just seemed to absorb him. One minute he was there, the next he was not. Even after all these years, I can find no better way to describe it.

The rest of us dismounted, took out our rifles and bellied up to the brow of the low hill. There I scanned the distant trees, wishing I had John Horan's telescopic sight with me. For ten long minutes we hunkered there and waited, and cursed the waiting.

Then there was a brief volley of gunfire that made more roosting birds rise up into the greying sky. The shots rolled out across the high plains. Two or three more shots jumbled together to form one messy, violent barrage. As the echoes died, I thought I heard a man loose off a throaty yell, but the distance was too great and I wasn't sure.

I hated the inactivity. I wanted to continue and conclude the chase. It was stupid, I know, stupid and immature, but I wanted to see John Kidd smile on the other side of his face when I gave him back that ten thousand dollar note and then took him in to Fort Wray.

Another shot rolled across the wide open country, but this time I recognised the higher cough of a handgun. Another shot followed it, and then one more. Unless I was much mistaken, this was the signal Winch had promised us.

We swung up into our saddles and came around the low hill at a run, bending forward so that the necks of our horses would give us some protection just in case it wasn't Winch who had signalled. Henry Morse led Winch's Roman-nosed pony.

But we needn't have worried. A big man in buckskins came striding out of the timber almost as soon as we came into sight, and it was surely our companion. He raised his Sharps high above his head and waved it back and forth.

Our horses ate up the ground and within moments we were drawing them down to a slithering, turf-tearing halt before the older man. Winch watched us come, standing hipshot and chewing on a fresh cube of cut-plug. He did not need me to ask him what had happened. His report came as brief and succinct as ever. "Left one man behind 'em, cap'n. I got 'im."

"Dead?"

He slapped the brass butt-plate of his carbine. "You shoot a man with this baby," he said proudly, "an' he stays shot."

I indicated the woods with a tilt of the jaw. "Let's see him."

He tucked his carbine back into the boot, mounted his pony from the right, Indian fashion, and led us at a walk deeper into the timber. Song sparrows and larks accompanied our progress with sweet, natural music, and the river chuckled and gurgled lazily by a couple of hundred yards further on. Without warning he reined in and pointed. A man with one of the most openly cruel faces I had ever seen was sitting up against the bole of a Douglas fir with his head hanging to one side and his eyes open wide in shock. His hat had fallen off to reveal his thinning blond hair, and there was blood all over his chest. His horse was tethered some little distance away, and the man himself was still clutching his repeater, even in death.

I looked at him for a long moment before I finally said, "The Butcher."

Henry Morse said, "Eh?"

"The one they called the Butcher of Belleville. Ryan." I turned my attention back to Winch. "The others?"

He hooked a thumb towards the Arikaree. "Found some tracks leadin' into the river."

"Think they swum across, Lem?" asked Yarbrough.

Winch shrugged. "Across. Upriver. Downriver. Came out further along this side or th'other. Can't say."

"Think you could pick up their tracks?" I asked.

He glanced up at the overcast beyond the canopy of twisted tree-limbs and spat a stream of tobacco juice onto the ground. "Light's failin'. Rain on the way." He looked back at me. "Lessen they's a special saint that looks after mantrackers, I'd say we've lost 'em, cap'n."

Behind me Henry Morse swore softly and his saddle creaked as he shifted around a little. I crossed my hands on my saddle-horn. What were we going to do now? I wondered. We'd had our one chance to trap Kidd and it had come to naught. Or had it? We still had one admittedly tenuous link to Kidd back at the ranch — Kansas Bill Johnson.

I directed Saul and Henry to load the body across his horse and told them that we were getting back before the rain started. When Saul asked if he should wrap the dead man in his blanket, I shook my head.

"When we ride back in, I want Kansas Bill to see him just the way he looks right now," I said harshly. "There's no more powerful inducement to get a man talking than the sight of a dead comrade."

I sounded confident as I said it, but deep down inside I wasn't so sure. Once again, I had no choice in the matter save to wait and see, and hope that I would be proved correct.

6

THE sky darkened further as the clouds I had first seen balancing atop the far blue mountains came down onto the flats, and the rain itself caught up with us before we had gone half a mile. Hastily we untied and donned our slickers, then continued on our way.

We must have looked a grim band when we finally rode back into Buckhalter's yard forty minutes later, our high-stepping horses moving slowly and with their big heads down, the men and I all but lost beneath our crackling yellow oilskins, sitting slumped and huddled in wet saddles, with water dripping steadily from our hat-brims.

It was some time around midday, but already lamplight was showing at the windows of the main house.

Glancing that way, I wondered how Ed Buckhalter was faring. I had seen wounds such as his many times before. I myself had been shot during a gunfight only a few months earlier. Though Buckhalter would be hurting worse than he'd ever thought possible, the pain *would* pass, and once the bullet was cut out of him, his body would begin the slow process of healing itself.

We walked our horses into the barn and dismounted. Down at the far end, a closed lantern threw a dusky glow out across Bob Bancroft and, stretched out on a rough pallet of hay at his feet, Kansas Bill Johnson. Johnson was conscious, though obviously in great discomfort and pain. He was craning his neck to get a better look at us. I passed my reins over to Winch and walked down there to join them, keeping my movements slow and deliberate in order to intimidate this Johnson in much the same way that he had tried to intimidate Buckhalter.

The rain came down harder. It beat

against the walls with a rattle like thunder and dripped through one or two holes in the roof in perforated silver lines. The horses shifted around, uneasy with the savagery of the storm, and the smell of blood and death.

I did not immediately acknowledge the outlaw's presence there on the floor, but instead concentrated my attention on Bancroft. "Has Horan gone?" I asked softly.

He nodded. "Cleared out just after you left," he replied. "Then Ruthie sent one of Buckhalter's men for a doctor."

I looked at him in the lamplight and even though it was none of my affair I couldn't help thinking, *Oh, it's Ruthie, is it?* I said, "Buckhalter all right?"

"Should be. They winged 'im, is all." He turned his bright, keen hazel eyes on all the activity behind me and said, "Any luck?"

"We got Dave Ryan," I answered, and saw Johnson start beneath his grubby, threadbare blanket.

Turning, I nodded to Yarbrough, who led the death-horse down to our end of the barn and then dutifully fetched out a knife and cut the pigging strings holding the dead man in place, just as we had prearranged.

The body fell heavily from the saddle and landed on the dirt floor with a loose thud, then rolled so that it was stretched out on its back, glassy eyes staring, face flecked with blood, raindrops showing like tears on the cold, pale cheeks, caked blood and chewed flesh visible through the ripped chambray shirt.

I was struck then by the realisation that Dave Ryan had already ceased to be a person to me. Death had a way of doing that, of robbing a man's identity from him. He was no longer a *he* to me, he had become an *it*.

Kansas Bill's sick-looking eyes were like two saucers as he identified his erstwhile companion. He was a tall, gangling man. It was hard to put an age to him, but he was around twenty eight or nine I supposed, with a thin, sallow face and whiskers and long, fuzzy sideburns a shade lighter than the chestnut of his long, matted hair.

I looked into his face. It wasn't hard to see that the sight of Ryan's corpse had rattled him. I knelt, the better to address him, and when he looked back at me I saw something guarded come into his eyes and I knew that this was going to be anything but easy.

"You and your friends have got a hideout somewhere in these parts," I said. "I want to know where it is."

Despite the pain of his hip-wound, he forced a chuckle, worked up some spit and let it go in a stream off to one side. "You can go to hell!"

Patiently I came at it from a different direction. "Tell me about the rustling, Bill."

"What rustlin'?" he croaked guilelessly.

"Come on now, Bill. Let's not beat around the brush. I know your reputation — blackmail, robbery, rustling, murder. You're hellbent for a hangrope, my friend. Unless . . . "

He read my mind. "If you think I'd sell my pals down the river, you don't know me a-tall, mister."

"You'll tell me everything I want to know," I said, trapping his feverish eyes with my own. "And you'd better tell me fast, because we haven't got the time to wait for you to see sense."

Again he rasped, "Go to hell!"

I sighed. "I'll get it all out of you sooner or later, Bill. Why don't you make it easy on yourself?"

"Easy on *you* is what you mean!"

I tufted. "Now just you think for a moment. There's not a court in the land that won't show clemency to a man who shows remorse and cooperates with the law. You give me what I want and you have my word that I'll speak up for you at your trial."

He was disparaging. "An' what'll that get me? Life, 'stead of hangin'? You'd hafta do a whole lot better'n that, mister!"

I straightened up again. This was

getting us nowhere. But the slurring of his voice had given me an idea. "You're tired," I said. "And that's too bad, because you're not going to get any rest until you tell us what we want to know." I fixed Bancroft with a stern eye. "Wake him up every time he looks like dozing off."

Bancroft looked sharply at me. He opened his mouth to speak but I talked him down. "*Do* it, Bob," I said, and turning to face the others, I told them to do the same thing when it came their turn to watch our prisoner.

Johnson stammered, "H-hey now . . . "

Glancing over my shoulder I said, "It doesn't have to come to that, if you cooperate."

"Damn you, you son-of-a-bitch. You'll get nothin' outta me!"

I shrugged. "We'll see."

I hated to do it, of course. I took no pleasure in making this man's situation any worse than it already was, no matter what he might have done in the past to deserve it. But it was as I had told him time was at a premium, and he was our only lead to John Kidd. We needed all the information he could give us, because without it we could scour this country for a year or more and still never find our man.

I saw Saul Yarbrough pondering what I had said. At last he spoke up, lifting his voice to be heard above the downpour. "I don't cotton much to breakin' a man's spirit like that, Mr Colter."

I wanted to say to him, *And you think I do?* Instead I said, "All he's got to do is tell us what we want to know."

"I'd as soon have no part in it."

My breath came out in a hiss. "Well, that's up to you. You can always quit." But I didn't want him to, so I added in a more conciliatory tone, "Sometimes we have to do things we don't care for. That's life."

I went over to my horse, off-saddled, wiped him down and turned him into a stall. Around us the storm struck at the barn and when the wind picked up it made the weathered boards creak. The men never once took their eyes off me. Perhaps they were hoping that I would relent. But how could I? We had to have that information, at practically any cost.

I tossed my horse a couple of forkfuls of good grass hay and finally said, "You be all right with it, Bob?"

He held back a moment before responding. It was in none of our natures to commit what amounted to an act of torture upon another man. But at last he nodded. "It's got to be done, I reckon."

I nodded brusquely, then pulled my slicker tighter around me and headed out into the rain, figuring to see how Ed Buckhalter was doing.

* * *

I hoped that Bill Johnson would see sense. Either that, or he would be too weak a man to hold out for very long.

149

But somehow he held out for forty eight hours.

Two full days. And in such pain, too. My God.

One of Buckhalter's men fetched a doctor out from Fort Wray. The doctor operated first on Buckhalter, and then on our prisoner. For a time there was nothing we could do but let him rest, despite what I had said to the contrary. But as soon as his morphine-induced narcosis wore off, we set about our onerous task of depriving him of his sleep.

I took my share at it, and I hated it every bit as much as did my companions. There in the cold gloom at the back of the barn I watched him moan and whine beneath his blanket, begging for rest. His dark eyes sank deeper into his skull and turned wild. It was then, when we felt that he might be about to break, that I or one of the others would lean forward and almost beg him in return to cooperate and tell us all he knew. But every time he would simply curse us and then fall quiet for a while.

It was exhausting just to watch him fighting so hard to hold out against the inevitable. I came out of the barn after my first shift feeling twice my age, for it was a wretched, soul-destroying chore I had brought about. But finally he broke — he broke and when he did it was like watching a dam burst, because he told us everything we wanted to hear and more besides.

He told us that the rustled stock was held in a small box canyon about fifty miles east of the Buckhalter place. Kidd kept a couple of men there who were skilled in the art of altering brands — brand blotchers, as we called them back then. From there the cattle were pushed southeast into Kansas in a series of small, manageable herds. There was a man in the Smoky Hills country who bought everything Kidd could bring him. Kidd even owned one of the small ranches along the trail, and paid hush-money to various of his neighbours in order to keep the operation a secret.

Once I had it all, I turned to Winch and asked him if he knew the box canyon Johnson had mentioned. He paused in his tobacco chewing for a moment and pulled at one of his pendulous ear lobes. "Iffen it's there, I c'n find it," he allowed.

I nodded. "All right. Saul, we'll need provisions. Go see what Miss Buckhalter can spare us. Henry, go with him. Bob — you'd better stay behind and keep an eye on Johnson."

I could see in his eyes that he hated to miss out on whatever action might be coming, but when he still said nothing and just accepted his orders with a curt nod, I revised my opinion of him again, although sourly I wondered if I were misunderstanding his motives, that in reality he was secretly pleased to have the opportunity of spending more time with Ruth Buckhalter . . . his 'Ruthie'.

"How long do you s'pose you're

gonna be gone?" he asked.

"I can't say, at this stage. If Kidd's already flown the coop, we'll go after him." I thought about it for a moment, then pointed to Johnson, who was already drifting off into a long-postponed slumber. "The doctor says he shouldn't be moved for about a week. If we're not back by then, and this business done with, I want you to take him into town and get him locked up. The minute we catch Kidd, I'll wire you care of the Cattlemen's Association and let you know."

I set about readying my horse for travel, all too aware that, while I had revised my opinion of Bancroft, my men had revised their opinion of *me*. There was no doubt that I had lost my standing with them because of the repulsive treatment I had prescribed for Johnson. And to make the matter worse, Ruth had also turned distinctly chilly towards me, once she had come to learn of it.

But I thrust all of that from my

mind. I had to. I was not here to win their favour. We had a job to do. Again I felt the outline of the folded ten thousand dollar note in my pocket. It was a constant reminder to me that John Kidd was still at large, and taunting me for my feeble attempts to bring him to book.

We left the Buckhalter place an hour later and rode steadily southeast through the bitter day. I wondered if we would catch our man at the box canyon. I doubted it. Now that he knew for sure that someone was after him, Kidd would probably leave this neck of the woods, at least for a while.

We rode right through the day and would have gone further but for the early darkness. With heavy, drifting clouds blotting what little light the moon and stars might otherwise have provided, we had little option but to call a halt. We found a high, protected spot and made camp, and an hour before dawn the next morning, Winch rode out to scout the terrain ahead.

We rode out after him about an hour later and spied him coming back towards us across the lonely, treeless plain some ten miles further on.

"Found the canyon, cap'n," he said when finally he brought his ugly horse to a halt and leaned forward with his arms folded atop his saddlehorn.

I could tell from his tone that he had only bad news for us. "They've gone?"

"Musta lit out two days ago. But they're trailin' a herd fifty, sixty-strong, an' not jus' cattle, neither. Hosses as well. So they won't be hard to foller — long as the weather holds, that is."

"They headin' for Kansas?" asked Saul.

"I reckon."

We rode for the canyon, reached it around the middle of the windswept day, paused briefly for coffee and a bite to eat, then set off after the rustlers and their stolen stock. The miles hurried past beneath us. Ten, twelve, fifteen, twenty. I cannot tell you exactly when we crossed the border. The land did not change greatly in character. It remained largely treeless and flat, with endless plains of buffalo or grama grass shelving away on every side. But the weather *did* change — for the worse. The temperature plummeted, for winter was now grasping the land with its icy hand, and that same afternoon we had a light powdering of snow.

Now we rode more cautiously, well aware that Kidd paid some of the farmers and ranchers in these parts for their silence and, possibly, whatever information they considered might be important to him. Whenever we spotted any signs of civilisation, we went out of our way to avoid being seen. Neither could the possibility of an ambush be entirely dismissed.

We rode on, single-minded and steadfast, trending eastwards now. The days turned greyer and colder. The freezing air rasped against my lungs like sandpaper and left all of us feeling numb and heavy-headed. Around the middle of the third day we spotted a huddle of clapboard and tarpaper buildings on the far northern horizon, what passed for a town in this part of the country.

Although we were low on supplies, I was reluctant to delay. Still, I knew we must replace what we had used up, and so, as mindful as ever of the need for circumspection, I sent only one man, Saul, in to buy supplies, while Winch, Morse and I made for a patch of ground about a mile away that was protected from the wind by a stand of cottonwoods and box elders.

We waited largely in silence, Winch chewing and spitting, Morse humming softly and stamping his feet, me holding my mustang's reins and staring out over the empty desolation, as introspective as ever.

I was much troubled. I did not want to be chasing across the country with winter closing in around us. I still cherished my dream of a more settled, less violent life, of a horse-ranch, a wife and a family. And yet I knew I must go on and see this thing through to the finish, and not just for the money. Pride was involved here as well.

The sky grew more and more bleak. There was another light powdering of snow. I wanted to finish this business and be done with it. But how? By the time Saul rejoined us with bulging saddlebags, I had reached a decision.

We were going to abandon our pursuit, and instead make directly for Kidd's likeliest destination — his ranch.

The men exchanged a glance once I had voiced my intention. Only Winch showed no real surprise, for I suspect he had already guessed what was in my mind. According to Johnson, Kidd's ranch was down along the Saline River. Now I said, "How far is the Saline from here, Lem?"

Scratching his wiry grey beard, he considered. "Ten, fifteen miles south."

I nodded. "All right. Let's cook up

some coffee, boys. Then we'll move out."

We picked up the Saline late in the day and from there we rode on eastwards, following the contortions of its sluggish flow. My stomach turned sour every time I thought about the showdown that must come when we raided the ranch. We had no idea how large a force we would encounter there, but we were certain to be outnumbered. I wondered briefly about the chances of contacting the county sheriff and trying to organise some reinforcements, but there was no way of knowing just whom we could trust. To have owned a ranch out here for so long and remain undetected, it seemed likely that even the sheriff was on Kidd's payroll.

We were on our own, then.

At last I judged that we were closing upon our destination. As the premature darkness crowded down upon us, I sent Winch out ahead to scout around and report back.

The others and I reined in among

some sparse timber. The day was biting and damp, and as one we felt wretched with the cold. We built a small fire and huddled around it, warming our rough palms and stamping our frozen feet. Snowflakes began to tumble lazily from the heavens above, and we listened to them hiss and sizzle as they connected with the greedy flames.

Some hours later Winch drifted soundlessly back into the firelight, and Henry filled a steaming mug for him. He told us that Kidd had already reached the ranch. He had checked on some of the cattle grazing beyond the buildings and found freshly doctored brands that were healing nicely. Then he picked up a stick and swiftly sketched an outline of the place in the loamy soil, and we gathered around and listened intently as he identified the main house, the bunkhouse, two sheds, a barn, corral and windmill.

"You reckon that's the same stock Kidd pushed up from Colorado, then?" asked Henry.

Winch spat into the fire, creating a vicious sizzle. "I'd say. That's prime stock, but ribby an' tired. Been pushed hard, an' recent."

I set my own mug aside. "Any idea how many men there were?"

"Di'n't like to get too close, 'cause they wuz havin' 'emselves some kinda wing-ding, an' the ranch wuz lit up like the Fourth o' July. Feller with a fiddle, 'nother with a squeeze-box . . . sounded to me like they wuz lettin' off a little steam, havin' reached trail's-end."

I was inclined to agree with him. As far as Kidd was concerned, nobody other than his confederates knew of his involvement with the spread. He and his men doubtless felt safer there than anywhere else.

I sat back once he had finished, and ran everything I had heard through my mind. So they were celebrating, were they? With any luck, that would make our job easier, for they would be sore-headed and in no mood to make much of a fight of it when we finally braced them.

The men were watching me. I looked back at them and reached my decision. "All right," I said. "Bed down while you've got the chance. We're pulling out again just after midnight."

Saul Yarbrough's question was direct. "What's the plan, Mr Colter?"

I pointed at the hieroglyphics Winch had made in the earth. "We're most likely to find Kidd and his men here, in the main house, or here, in the bunkhouse. So that's where we'll concentrate our attention. We'll raid the place at dawn, while they're still sleeping off tonight's drink. Once we've got the drop on them, it's just the question of disarming them and then tying them up."

"What if they've posted guards?" asked Henry.

I glanced speculatively at Winch. He said, "I spotted one man ridin' night-herd while I wuz there. Di'n't spot nobuddy else."

I had long-since learned to trust his judgment in such matters, and was satisfied with that. "Can you take care of any guards or nighthawks before we get into position?"

He fingered the Green River skinning knife in a sheath on his belt, and his grin was wicked and filled with relish. "Consider it done," he said with a cackle.

I turned back to the others. "Henry, you and Lem will take the bunkhouse. Saul, you and I will take the main house. If we can do this without firing a shot, so much the better. You know how I feel about killing. But let's have no doubts — if any one of them tries to make a fight out of it, we've got no choice in the matter — it's us or them."

They nodded and muttered agreement.

I drew in a deep, cold breath. The plan was made, and there was no going back on it. We were committed.

"Get some sleep," I advised again . . . and wondered if any of us would.

At least one of us did. I lay there in my blankets and listened to Winch's low, regular breathing for hours. I listened to him, and to the restless tossings and turnings of the other two.

At last I reached down, took out my pocket watch and tilted it towards the fire. It was eleven-thirty. I got up with a shiver, refilled the coffee pot and set it atop one of the rocks at the fire's edge.

Gradually Saul and Henry threw back their blankets and sat up. There was no talk. They dry-washed their faces, helped themselves to coffee, sat there blowing on the brew and listened to Winch's heavy, relaxed breathing.

I checked my handgun and rifle. Saul and Henry followed my example. It started snowing again. We set about saddling up. An owl flapped through the branches above us, searching for food, and a moment later, not far off, a small animal squealed piteously, then fell silent.

My horse saddled, I kicked dirt onto what remained of the fire, then bent to rouse Winch. Before I got anywhere near him, however, his voice came out from beneath his blanket. "I'm awake."

He got up, stretched, gathered his gear together and went across to his horse. He readied it, then came back and said, "I'll go on ahead. Kidd's place's about a dozen miles further along the river. They's a stand o' willow trees jus' this side of it. When you reach 'em, stay there. Don't go no further till I come back an' fetch you."

We all muttered our goodbyes and good lucks, and then he heeled the pony off into the darkness. A few minutes later we mounted up and set off in the same direction. Moonlight spilled through a gap in the clouds, back-lighting the snow so that it seemed to glow as it see-sawed to earth. An hour hurried past. Our walking horses ate up about four miles. The timber thinned and we found ourselves following a scrub-littered riverbank ever eastwards. The only sounds were the plodding of our horses, the creak of our saddles, the odd sigh from my companions or I.

At last the willows Winch had mentioned rose up before us through the early-morning darkness. I twisted around and gestured that we should dismount and walk our mounts the rest of the way.

We settled in among the willows and waited. The blustery wind pushed their graceful, flexible branches this way and that. The horses stamped, restless. Melting snow turned our shoulders and hats dark.

The waiting was a trial, as waiting always is. But mercifully it did not last long, for within a quarter of an hour, Winch suddenly materialised beside me and hissed, "It's done, cap'n. Jus' the one nighthawk, like I tol' you."

"You *kill* 'im, Lem?" asked Saul in a low, awe-struck voice.

"Wal," Lem replied casually, "Let's put it this way. He shore won't be singin' them beeves to sleep no more."

I shivered. "All right, men. Tie your horses."

We tethered our mounts and hauled out our rifles. I told Lem to lead on, and he light-footed back the way he had come and we fell in behind him. Abruptly the willows thinned and we went down behind some patchy brush to survey the ranch beyond.

It looked run-down and well-seasoned — in short, just like any other ranch. The buildings were mere bulks of shadow, some large, some not so large, all of plank and shingle construction. They gathered around the central yard like mountain men at a rendezvous.

Everything was in darkness. The blustery breeze made the windmill turn with a scraping, laddery sound, but other than that, there was no sound and no movement. I glanced up at the sky and saw the faintest hint of a new day etching the eastern horizon. I looked at the others. Their faces mirrored my own tension. I whispered,

"Ready?" and they nodded to show that they were.

Lem said, "You fellers do like me — an' don't go makin' no noise."

He held back for a moment, then broke cover. He crouch-ran from the brush across the patchy grass and scrub until he was lost among the shadows of the nearest shed.

We held our breath, half-expecting that someone would hear him and raise the alarm, but no-one did.

Henry went next, and when he was safely across, I touched Saul on the arm and the big black man broke cover and ran for the first of the buildings. Within seconds I had joined him.

When we had our breath back, we split up. Saul and I crossed over to the other side of the yard while Lem and Henry stayed where they were. We reached the shadows around the barn and went down into a crouch. Still nothing moved around us, save for the odd stamping of a horse deep inside the barn, or the stray, natural sounds of settling boards.

We watched Lem and Henry creep slowly but surely towards the low bunkhouse a hundred yards ahead, then followed their lead and set off towards the main house, which was no more than sixty or seventy yards from our position. We had allowed ourselves a quarter of an hour to reach our respective stations, but our progress was so painstaking that I wondered if we would reach them in time.

At last we reached the house. As we had previously agreed, Saul began to skirt around to the front and I to edge around to the rear. A stack of garbage had grown up at the side of the place and I heard rats scuttling around within its damp, noxious confines.

Finally I came around the corner and halted at the back of the property, staring up at its blank windows and listening for any signs of life inside. We had been at this business of skulking around in the dark for what seemed like forever, and away to the east, the sky was getting lighter all the while.

Stepping closer, I chanced a quick glance in through one of the small windows. Beyond my own pale reflection, the interior was just a pool of ink.

My throat felt tighter now, and breathing was an effort. Not for the first time, I felt that my body was trying to rebel against the violent course upon which I had set myself. But time was wasting. I could not afford distraction now. With my pulses hammering, I reached down, closed my fingers around the door-handle, twisted it gently . . .

It gave with the smallest of clicks. I held onto it for a moment. Sweat was dribbling down my face, despite the cold. When nothing happened, I took a chance and pushed the door wider. It creaked softly, but not enough to arouse any of the occupants from their deep, drink-induced slumber.

I entered the kitchen.

I couldn't make out much more than the basics — a zinc-lined sink and pump, the sink stacked with cups and dishes; a dark, bulky-looking range in which embers still glowed faintly orange; some cupboards.

A narrow, curtained aperture in the facing wall led into the parlour. Cautiously, rifle grasped in clammy hands, I pushed through it.

Entirely without warning then, a gunshot ripped the pre-dawn stillness asunder.

7

I KNEW it hadn't come from anywhere close by, so my immediate thought was, *The bunkhouse.*

In the same moment, the front door slammed open and I saw a big man outlined in the gap. I yelled, *"Don't shoot, Saul, it's me!"*

Elsewhere in the house, a woman screamed. Men were yelling as well, both here and on the other side of the yard. Another flurry of gunshots erupted over by the bunkhouse. I didn't know what could have happened, save that something somewhere had gone wrong for us, and that Lem and Henry might very badly be in need of our help.

A window smashed. It sounded as if it came from one of the rooms to my left. I shouted for Saul to go and help Lem and Henry, then spun around, ran back through the kitchen and burst outside.

I was right. A man in red longjohns and pants, barefoot and with gunbelt, boots and shirt coiled in a ball under one arm, was trying to make his getaway through a back bedroom window. He came through the side of the house in a shower of glass and hit the ground running. We collided, grunted and went down in a tangle of arms and legs. He threw his gear into my face, then put his hands around my throat and started strangling me.

I shook my head furiously to clear his belongings out of my face, let go of my rifle, brought my arms up inside his and then flung them outwards, to break his hold. He took a swipe at me, struck me on the side of the head. My hat came off and we rolled into all the garbage.

The sky was lightening swiftly now, and we rolled some more through the greyness until he came out on top, pinned my arms to the ground with his knees and got his fingers around my throat once more.

I bucked like a wild horse, but could not immediately dislodge him. Then, in one feverish moment that sticks in my memory even at this late date, my eyes finally focused upon him.

I was not apt to forget John Kidd's face. It had haunted me ever since that night at The Mother Lode. When our eyes met, he seemed to recognise me too. Then, with a roar, I lifted my right shoulder and, caught off-balance, he tumbled sideways.

The pair of us struggled desperately then to be the first one back on his feet. I heard a noise behind me, another man, yelling something, and corkscrewed around and down all in one motion. The newcomer, I saw, was racing out through the back door, equally dishevelled, and brandishing a Colt revolver.

The gun boomed and a foot-long spear of orange flame spat at me. Once again instinct took over and my right hand swept down towards the .442 at my hip. All at once the weapon filled my hand, blurred up, spoke some thunder of its own, and the other man hunched up, called out something, stumbled sideways like a drunk and then toppled over.

Behind me, I heard racing footsteps. Kidd was getting away! I turned, bawled, *"Hold it!"* But he had no intention of stopping, he just kept running, having retrieved some of his scattered gear.

I raised my gun, fired once more over his head. He broke stride but then, realising that I had not hit him, picked up speed again.

"Hold it, damn you!"

He kept running, heading for the brush at the back of the property.

I tilted the .442 so that it was centred on a point between his shoulder-blades and took up the first pressure —

Someone crashed into me from behind and I was punched earthward again. We hit the dirt in a jumble, and a flurry of blows caught me in the face and made me screw my eyes shut. We rolled, I came out on top, jabbed my gun straight into the other man's face and husked, *"Hold it right there — you're under arrest!"*

I saw then that I had not been attacked by another man. This was a woman — probably the very same woman who had screamed when the first of the gunfire had erupted. She glared up at me, her dark brown eyes twin pools of fiery hatred, her bottom lip trembling with anger.

My respect for women had long been ingrained into me, and automatically now I stood up and stepped back from her. Still, I could not help gaping. Her thin, diaphanous nightgown offered practically nothing in the way of cover for her at all, and her curved figure was revealed clearly beneath the thin, impractical material.

She was not armed — not that I could see — and apart from her initial attack, I did not see her as any real danger. I looked around. There was no sign of Kidd. But there was still a constant and worrisome rattle of gunfire coming from the front of the house, so I stuffed my handgun away, snatched up my rifle and hurried around there to lend a hand.

The yard looked more like a battlefield. Two men lay in the dirt, one still, the other trying to claw his way painfully back towards the bunkhouse, still twenty feet away.

Muzzle-flashes winked at me from some of the shattered bunkhouse windows, and hurriedly I threw myself down behind a water-butt to one side of the porch. I flinched as bullets punched into the far side of the barrel. Then, after it went quiet again, but for the sound of water emptying out through the bullet-holes, I raked my surroundings for sign of my companions.

The first man I spotted was Saul Yarbrough. He was kneeling behind a trough opposite the bunkhouse, sighting carefully, then firing his Winchester every time he caught a movement inside the building. A bit further away, firing into the bunkhouse from behind a pile of cut logs, was Henry Morse.

I thought about the situation we had gotten ourselves into, and wondered how we were going to resolve it.

The wounded man was still dragging himself towards the bunkhouse, slithering inchmeal like some gigantic snake, and leaving a slimy trail of blood in his wake. Suddenly he just stopped moving and lay there with his face in the dust, and I knew with a sick feeling that death had just overtaken him, that I had actually seen him die.

I wondered then if all the shooting and killing would *ever* end.

Lem Winch caught my attention from the other side of the yard at just that moment. He had somehow worked his way down between one of the sheds and the outhouse, and now he yelled, "The barn, cap'n! Couple of 'em got inta the barn!"

Even as he said it and I spun that way, there came an ominous rumble and suddenly the big barn doors juddered open and horses streamed out in a wild, rushing torrent.

Riderless and half scared to death by all the gunfire, the first of them wheeled left and came racing right through the centre of the yard with the remainder — upwards of thirty animals — following blindly on at a frenzied gallop.

The yard was hurled into absolute chaos. The ground trembled beneath their crashing hooves and the noise was deafening. The horses flooded past in a fast-flowing river of blacks, browns and paints — and there, right in the middle of them all, I spotted three half-dressed men huddling low in hastily-cinched saddles.

"*There!*"

I came up, snap-aimed at one of the outlaws and fired my rifle. He twitched and slumped backwards, but somehow managed to hold onto his horse's reins and stay in the saddle.

He fetched a big black handgun around on me. I levered my rifle — a good, reliable Yellow Boy — and shot at him again. I missed. His horse was moving too fast, and because he was swaying about so violently, he was a hard target.

But that didn't matter, for he finally lost his balance and slipped from the back of his horse with a horrified scream. He struck the earth so forcefully that he actually bounced a little against the hardpan. Then the rest of the horses ran over him, carried him along a short way, broke him, pulped him.

The last of the horses left the yard behind them. They would run for miles and then scatter to every point of the compass. All that was left at the ranch was a kind of shocked silence and dead or near-to-dead men.

With effort I found my voice and called upon the men still holed up in the bunkhouse to surrender. There was no response. We waited for a time, as the weak, hazy sun slowly strengthened. I think we all knew that those men who had been pinned down in there had long-since used all the confusion to make their escape.

Saul came out from behind the trough. No-one shot at him. Carefully he approached the bunkhouse, long gun at the ready. The rest of us hardly dared to breathe as we watched him. He made it as far as the half-open, bullet-chewed door, and used the rifle barrel to push it wider. He went inside. A moment later he came back out and confirmed what we had already half-guessed.

"They' gone, Mr Colter. Left one dead man behind 'em, an' a feller nursin' a busted wing."

I came up straight. "All right. Rest of you men okay?"

Saul I already knew about. Winch called over, "Ayuh." Henry came across from the log-pile looking sheepish.

"I'm sorry, Mr Colter," he said, obviously angry with himself. "I bollixed this up for you, an' no mistake. Got around to the back of the bunkhouse quiet as you like. Then my boot caught on an empty whiskey bottle, an' all hell busted loose."

I told him to forget it. What else could I say? He had been game to come along in the first place. After all, this was not his usual line of work. He was a cowboy, not a manhunter.

I had Saul and Henry patch up the wounded man as best they could and then keep watch on him until we could take him in to the nearest town and hand him over to the authorities. I sent Lem back to fetch our mounts. There was no point in trying to pursue the rest of the outlaws — they, like their horses, would have scattered by now.

I checked out the main house. The remnants of the previous night's party were sour reminders of better times past. I went through the kitchen and out into the backyard. The girl who had stopped me from shooting Kidd was kneeling beside the first man I had killed. She had dragged a coat over the nightgown and her head was bent, so that her long black hair hung down over her face.

I knew she was crying.

I looked down at the dead man. Al Tate. After a moment, the girl looked up at me, and as the hair fell back from her face, I studied her closer in the grey daylight.

I judged her to be somewhere in her early twenties. She had a round, coppered face with small, attractive features. But her brown eyes, her full, slightly pouting mouth — even the aggressive tilt of her nose — spoke of rawhide toughness and fierce determination. She was of a hardy, stubborn breed, I could tell — and yet there was something tender in her too; something she tried to keep well-hidden.

She palmed the tears off her cheeks, her movements sharp and jerky, as if she were angry that someone else had been here to see her shed them. She looked at me for a long moment. Then she said, "You'd be Colter."

I was surprised. "You've heard of me?"

"John told me about you. About what happened in Fort Wray, the Buckhalter spread."

"You're Kidd's woman?"

She shrugged.

"Have you got a name?"

"Ella Morris."

"Where has he gone, Miss Morris?"

She laughed. It was a harsh, embittered bark. "You think I'd tell *you*?"

I pointed to the body at her bare feet. "This morning it was Al Tate, and those other men out front. Tomorrow it could be Kidd. Better we take him peacefully than he ends up shot to death."

Her eyes were tired and lifeless. "He'll die, one way or the other, when the law gets a-hold of him. At least while he's free, he's got a chance."

I couldn't argue with that. I looked at her. Again, I needed information, everything she could tell us. But she did not look like the sort who would give anything away.

I considered the position. What was I to do — starve her of her sleep until she broke and told us everything, just the way I had with Kansas Bill Johnson? No, I could not do that. I could not do that again to *anyone*, least of all a woman.

"Well," I muttered, "it probably won't count for much, but I regret what happened here today. I regret it very much."

She tilted her head to one side and looked at me. I felt uncomfortable under her brazen scrutiny. At length she said, "You're right. It doesn't count for one single, damned thing. But for what it's worth, I believe you mean what you say, mister."

I left her there with the body and went back through the gloomy, cluttered house. We had four dead men, aside from Al Tate, and one wounded, to identify. One was a brand blotcher by the name of Eli Pedersen. The second was a small, wiry man with bloodshot eyes called Norris. The third was a felon named Walter Braid, and the fourth was called McCain.

I went into the bunkhouse and questioned the wounded man. He was Jim Taylforth, the second of Kidd's brand blotchers. He was stretched out on a bunk midway down the low, dark room, clutching his shattered, blood-soaked shoulder and groaning through clenched teeth. Yes, I questioned him but he could tell us nothing save what we had already learned from Bill Johnson. He said he had no idea where Kidd might have gone to ground, and I believed him.

Frustrated, I went back outside and stood looking across the grassy flats. Clouds were gathering again, and it was cold enough for more snow. I felt glassy-eyed from lack of sleep, hollow from lack of food. I didn't know what we could possibly salvage from this affair. It had all gone so entirely wrong. Try as I might, I just could not think how we were going to pick up any further leads on our man's whereabouts.

Or *could* I . . . ?

Ella Morris was standing on the porch, watching me through dark, troubled eyes. I paid her no mind, but concentrated instead upon bringing some order to this shambles. Henry volunteered to see what he could throw together in the way of a meal and strode off in the direction of the cookshack behind the bunkhouse. Lem rode in, leading our horses. I took them from him, then told him to ride out and see if he could round up enough strays to help us pack the dead and wounded in to the nearest town.

Ella Morris was still watching me. Perhaps she was wondering if she was also a prisoner. She wasn't. Although she didn't know it, she was just about to become the bait.

We wrapped the dead men in their blankets and lay them out in a row before one of the sheds. Some time later, Lem herded four of the stray horses back into the yard, and we harnessed them up to the light wagon we had found inside the barn.

At length we were ready to go. By my reckoning, the nearest town of any consequence was Overton, which lay some forty miles to the north. I walked my mustang over to Ella Morris and looked down at her. She was dressed now, in a thick blue-wool dress and the coat, for the day was raw. I said, "Have you thought any more about what I asked you earlier?"

Her smile came out sour. "You'll not get John's whereabouts from me, Mr Colter."

There was no point in trying to persuade her. There was iron in her tone: she meant what she said. I put my fingertips to my hat-brim and said, "So long then, Miss Morris."

She watched us leave.

We rode for about five miles through a slanting, sleety rain before I called a halt and turned my horse to face the others. Saul and Henry were sitting on the high wagon seat, their horses tied to the tailgate. Jim Taylforth was squeezed in among the bodies, towards the rear of the coverless vehicle. "Saul, Henry — I want you to take these men on into town," I announced, reaching into my jacket pocket. "Here's my letter of introduction from the Cattlemen's Association. If the sheriff in Overton wants to confirm anything, you tell him all he's got to do is wire Simon Black."

They were all looking at me from beneath frowns, and the rain was making their eyelids flutter.

"What 'bout you an' me, cap'n?" asked Winch, curiosly.

"We're going back to the ranch," I said.

His eyebrows lifted. "You think Kidd's gonna chance goin' back there after the scare we thronged inta 'im this mornin'?" He shook his shaggy grey head. "Hell, he might be crazy, but he ain't that crazy."

"Well, the way I figure it, we're in with two chances, Lem. If Kidd won't come back to the woman, maybe the woman will go out to Kidd."

A slow grin moved the fuzz around his mouth. "You mean we let her lead us to him?"

"If we get lucky."

"What about us, Mr Colter?" asked Saul. "After we seen the sheriff, I mean?"

"Meet us back in that stand of willows just west of the ranch. Ride careful and make sure you're not seen. Take the long route around, just to make sure."

It was a long chance, I knew. But in the circumstances, I could think of nothing better, so Lem and I hauled our horses over to one side of the trail and waved the others on. We watched them until they were lost around the timbered bend, then turned our mounts back to the south.

We found a spot among the willows

and took turns in watching the ranch. The place remained quiet for what was left of the day. Every so often, Ella Morris came out to fetch wood or water, or just to stand before the house and survey the damage we had wrought. But nobody came, and nobody went, and when darkness fell, the windows of the main house lit up like lonely beacons.

The next day was the same. A couple of the horses wandered back into the yard, having run far enough and then lost all inclination save simply to return to their home ground. Ella fetched and carried, kept house, performed a hundred and one menial little tasks, inside and out. But still there was no sign of her beau or any of his men.

The weather turned murky. It remained damp, and mist wreathed in among the trees and brush. Saul and Henry rejoined us later that same day, having delivered their burden to the county sheriff. Still we kept a watch on Kidd's ranch.

It was a wretched, cold, uncomfortable time. We chanced a small, smokeless fire and took it in turns to eat half-cooked rations straight from the can, to drink stewed, thick black coffee and search for that elusive patch of dry ground upon which to spread our blankets and try to sleep.

"Do you think she's guessed that we're watching her?" I asked Lem on the third day.

He shook his head. He had more patience for this business than I. "Doubt it." Then he glanced at me and frowned. "Hey, cap'n — you feelin' all right?"

I blinked at him. "Sure."

"You look a mite peaked, is why I ask."

"I'm fine. Cold is all."

He accepted that and turned his attention back to the ranch. But in fact I was feeling ill. The unrelenting chill had given me a permanent headache, and my stomach had become a source of great discomfort to me.

On the morning of the fourth day, a band of riders came into the yard. Ella Morris came out to greet them, clutching a shawl around her firm, broad shoulders. Saul Yarbrough squinted at the newcomers and finally whispered, "See that big feller with the beard, Mr Colter? That's Dugan, the county sheriff."

This Dugan handed down a sheet of paper that Ella scanned briefly. There followed a heated exchange of words, and then Sheriff Dugan turned and addressed the men behind him. After that they turned their horses around and headed for the pastures beyond the house.

"I've a suspicion them other fellers'd be brand 'spectors," opined Henry in an undertone. "They musta come on out to confiscate the cattle."

He was right, for later that same morning we saw them hazing a sizeable herd of cattle south, to Overton. There they would be held in pens until representatives of Simon Black's

Association could arrive to identify them and prove ownership.

Six days later we were still no better off. Nobody came, nobody went, and nothing happened. Ella gave no indication that she was expecting visitors, and made no attempt to leave the ranch to go elsewhere. In all, we froze there in those willows for seven whole days, and all to no avail. In the end, I had no choice but to face the fact that we had lost Kidd yet again.

With some bitterness, we saddled up and headed for town. We had wasted a week. That was all I could think about. Our man could be halfway across the other side of the country by now, and most likely was.

But wasn't that just what he would expect us to think? Surely, he had always been renowned for doing what was *least* expected of him. So perhaps he *was* still in these parts, after all.

Once I started thinking along those lines, everything else fell into place and I began to formulate a plan that was not entirely to my liking, but which I felt might stand some reasonable chance of success.

We reached Overton, put our horses up at a stable and went to get our first bite of decent, home-cooked food in the better part of a month.

It was as we were lingering over coffee at a quiet corner table, and rainy dark was stealing across the sky outside, that Henry Morse said, "You' awful quiet all of a sudden, Mr Colter. Somethin' on your mind?"

I looked up and nodded. Keeping my voice low, even though there was scant chance of being overheard, I said, "I've been thinking. We need to get a man inside Kidd's gang."

"Kidd's gone, cap'n," Winch said regretfully. "That's a fact you can bank on in Denver."

"But what if he *isn't*?" I argued. "What if he was watching *us* while we were watching the ranch? Suppose he was only waiting for us to give up and ride away before he moved back in?"

They looked at me as if I were mad.

"Think about it," I said, warming to the subject now, as the notion took firmer hold in my brain. "Kidd's lost eight men. Six dead, if you include the nighthawk Lem put to sleep, and two wounded. He'll be looking to recruit again. If we could put *our* man in the gang . . ."

I watched them consider it.

"That'd be a risky proposition to put to a feller," Saul allowed, thoughtfully wiping the back of one hand across his mouth. "I mean, we've braced 'em twice now, Mr Colter. Ain't no tellin' jus' which of us they seen an' which of us they ain't. We send the wrong man in . . ."

"There's one man we know for a fact that they haven't seen," I replied, my eyes moving from one face to the next.

It was Winch who said it.

He whispered, "Bob Bancroft."

8

IT was, as Saul said, a risky proposition to put to a man, and I thought long and hard about it for what remained of the evening and most of the night that followed before I finally concluded that it was probably our only choice. Even if it came to nothing, it was at least worth a try.

First thing next morning, I wired Bob Bancroft in care of Simon Black's office, requesting that he come to Overton with all dispatch and meet with us at the hotel into which we had booked ourselves. Six days later, around the middle of the afternoon there was a knock on my room door and when I opened it, he was standing there in the hallway, saddlebags flung across one shoulder, his usual lazy, secretive grin pasted right across his handsome face.

The other men sprang up from their

chairs and came over to usher him inside. There followed a lengthy ritual of handshakes and slaps on back or arm, a few questions or comments upon the dire weather we were having. Then we all sat down again and as he dropped his saddlebags down on to the floor beside him he said, "Well, I knew you fellers couldn't do without me for long. What's the beef?"

It went quiet in the room, and leaning forward with my elbows on my knees, I brought him up to date with everything that had happened. At the finish, I told him about my idea of somehow getting a man into Kidd's gang, so that we might discover more about his movements and then make plans to be there ahead of him.

"A man," Bancroft mused, spilling Bull Durham tobacco onto a brown cigarette paper. "Me, huh?"

I looked him squarely in the face. His bright hazel eyes looked as keen and sardonic as ever. "I won't lie to you, Bob. It's not without its risks.

If Kidd *has* gone back to the ranch — and there's no telling for sure that he has — you'll have to convince him that you're an outlaw looking to find safety in numbers. You'll tell him that you heard about the trouble he had with us. That's why you made directly for his ranch. And you'll have to make it sound good, because if he should suspect that you're really working with *us* . . . well, it *could* turn nasty." I fell silent for a moment, then said carefully, "Do you understand what I'm saying?"

He brought the paper up to his lips, licked one edge and then rolled it into a narrow cylinder. Just before he tucked the cigarette into one corner of his mouth he said, "I understand."

"No man'd blame you if you said no, Bob," said Yarbrough.

I agreed. "Maybe you'd care to think about it for a while," I suggested. "You can let me know what you decide later this evening."

He struck a match and fired the

cigarette to life. "No need for that," he said. "I'm game for it."

I could hardly credit that he would treat such a serious undertaking in so cavalier a fashion. "You *do* understand the risks?" I said again.

"Ayuh."

"And you still feel confident enough to give it a go?"

"Ayuh."

I sat back. His attitude had taken all of us somewhat by surprise. "You fellers'll be ridin' herd on me, a'course," he said, breaking the silence.

I nodded, got up, went over to the dresser and opened a drawer. From out of it I took a small, oblong mirror I had bought the day before. "We'll be close by, and at least one of us will be watching at all times. If you need to get any information to us, find some excuse to slip outside and use this. The minute we see your signal, one of us will meet you down behind the outhouse. You can tell us what you've managed to find out then. In

200

the meantime, we've roughed out a map of the ranch, and directions how to get there. Once you've familiarised yourself with it, get rid of it, just in case."

He stood up and accepted the mirror. "Sounds reasonable." He looked around at the others and grinned, as if he found their obvious concern a source of great amusement. "All right, Mr Colter. I figure it's probably best if I don't see you fellers again for a while. I'll go take a look around town, have me an all-over bath an' get somethin' to eat, then pull out first light tomorrow. Fair enough?"

I nodded, gave him the map we had drawn, and offered my hand. "Best of luck, Bob," I said sincerely, and the other men echoed the sentiment.

"You jus' make sure you fellers're around iffen I need you," he replied lightly. "Oh, by the way, Mr Colter — Ruthie sends her regards."

I let go of his hand. Suddenly, irrationally, my attitude towards him

201

changed. Ruth Buckhalter. *Ruthie*. I had not entertained any romantic designs upon her at all, at least none that I was aware of. And yet I could not help envying him her company, and feeling jealous that he had been able to spend time with her when I had not.

His lazy smile widened slightly as I looked at him. It was almost as if he had said it deliberately, knowing how I would react.

He nodded to the others, clapped his big hat back on his dark blond head and strode towards the door.

★ ★ ★

We did not see him again. But early the following morning, having bought sufficient supplies for the duration of our stay in among the willows close to the ranch, the rest of the men and I assembled at the livery stable, saddled up and set out on a circuitous route that would lead us to our destination. The weather had not improved. It was dull and wet, the kind of weather that wreaks havoc upon a man's lungs if he stays out in it for too long. For myself, I still felt flushed and achy, and on the ride out, I lost count of the number of times I unhooked and drank from my canteen in an attempt to quench my permanent thirst.

Winch galloped out ahead to scout around. When he came back he reported that as far as he could see, Ella Morris was still living all alone at the ranch. Part of me hoped that it would stay that way, for Bancroft's over-confidence worried me, and I was concerned that Kidd might see through him, guess at his true purpose there and . . .

The consequences hardly bore consideration.

I had hoped never to see that wretched stand of willows ever again, and yet here we were once more, forced to live within its murky, sodden confines. We made the best kind of camp we could and worked out a system by which the ranch would be under constant scrutiny. After that it was simply a case of watching and waiting.

Halfway through the second watch I felt so sour in the stomach that I had to climb to my feet and stagger a few yards away so that I could be sick. I felt jumpy afterwards, for I desperately did not want to come down with anything, not now.

I ran a palm across my sweated face. I was burning up. I took another pull at my canteen. I was feeling giddy, and my mouth felt sticky and numb.

A noise drew me from my fevered tremblings, and I went down onto my still-rolling stomach and snaked back towards the screening brush. A man was chopping logs on the far side of the yard. It was Bancroft. *So far, so good, then*, I thought. He must have struck Ella as being sincere, otherwise I had no doubt that she would have ordered him off her land in no uncertain terms.

For three days we kept watch on the ranch. Bancroft made himself useful around the place, patching the roof, chopping more wood, exercising the horses, making good some of the damage we had caused during that earlier gun-battle.

Then, around nine o'clock that same evening, we suddenly caught the sound of hoofbeats and harness carrying on the wind, and as we climbed hurriedly to our feet, Henry Morse — whose turn it had been to keep watch on the ranch — came rustling back through the undergrowth, clutching his long gun.

All I could see of him through the darkness were the whites of his eyes and the brief flash of his teeth as he spoke. *"Riders!"* he hissed urgently. "Five of 'em." He swallowed hard and said, "I think it's Kidd an' his bunch."

As one, the rest of us grabbed our rifles and headed back through the sleeping timber, automatically going down on to our bellies as the willows thinned and were replaced by the tangled mesh of the brush.

We were lucky in that we had a reasonably unrestricted view of the ranch, and that the night was clear, so that moonlight bathed the place in a sallow shimmer.

As Henry had said, five horses had been tethered to the rack in front of the main house. Amber light fell in slanted blocks from the windows of the place. I studied the dwelling, my throat tight. Was Henry right? Had Kidd actually come back, as I had half-suspected and half-hoped he would? And if so, would he accept whichever yarn Bancroft spun to him, or would his suspicious nature predispose him against any newcomer?

I heard a low babble of conversation through the thin walls and patched windows, but it was indistinct and impossible to decipher. I was almost afraid to believe that Fate had actually given us another chance at Kidd. It was almost too good to be true. But then I cautioned myself. We did not know for a fact whether Kidd *had* come back, yet.

When it became obvious that nothing was going to happen immediately, I sent Lem and Saul back to camp to catch up on their rest, and told Henry to go along with them as well.

"You sure, Mr Colter?"

I nodded. "I'm sure. I'll keep watch for a while."

Left alone, I lay there squinting through the darkness, wondering what was going on inside the house, straining my ears to catch a word here or recognise a voice there.

I ran one hand over my mouth. It felt sore and inflamed.

An hour passed slowly. Trying desperately to remain optimistic, I took that as a good sign. The evening wore on. It grew darker, and the wind turned even more bitter. My eyes became glassy from so much staring, and I began to feel stiff and chilly again.

The hands of my pocket watch edged towards midnight. My eyelids drooped.

I wanted to stay awake, but I couldn't. My appetite had gone by this time, you see, and my constitution had weakened. I dozed off once and came awake with a start. Again I concentrated my attention upon the main house. Still nothing happened, and within ten minutes I was dozing again.

I dreamt of Ruth Buckhalter.

When next I awoke, snow was swirling and corkscrewing all around me. I felt groggy and ashamed that I had slept for so long. I pushed up onto my knees, and snow tumbled wetly from my shoulders.

I knuckled my eyes and squinted at the ranch. The horses were no longer tied out front. Most probably Kidd and his men had taken them into the barn and off-saddled. I checked the time. It was a little after two in the morning. Still the windows of the house were warmed by lamp-light.

I cleared my throat. I felt stiff and sore. I couldn't be certain, but it felt as if my tongue had swollen up.

I heard a sound behind me and twisted around, awkward in my bulky clothes. Saul Yarbrough came out of the darkness and crouched beside me, eyes slitted against the churning snow. "Go on back an' grab some coffee, Mr Colter," he said. "I'll take over here fo' a while."

I nodded, clapped him on the shoulder and staggered back to camp. My shoulders ached fiercely. I poured myself a mug of coffee and drank it down, for my thirst was as persistent as ever. Sitting cross-legged there beside the faintly glowing embers, I dozed again.

I snapped awake four hours later, not entirely sure where I was, or why. Then my glazed eyes cleared and I saw the other men moving around and memory came back.

I stood up and looked around. It had stopped snowing, and by the look of it, not a moment too soon. Snow and ice rimed every bush and branch. It had blanketed the entire countryside.

I shivered.

Saul came in, hugging himself to keep warm, and reported no change at the ranch. Silently Lem stalked off to take over the watch. I stumbled away through the trees until I was out of sight, then bent double and was violently sick.

Three hours later, Lem came back into camp, wearing a frown. "Somethin's wrong down at that there ranch, cap'n," he said. "I don't like the lookuvit."

With effort, I got to my feet. "What do you mean, something wrong?"

"Ain't seen nor heard no signs' a life. An' that lamp they got burnin' inside the house — it's still burnin'."

That *was* odd. Even though the day was overcast, there was no need to keep a lamp burning. With coal-oil the precious and expensive commodity that it was, most frontier people tried not to burn any more of it than they had to.

I grabbed up my rifle. "Take a look around," I said, and Lem nodded and turned away.

The rest of us tramped through the snow, back to the edge of the brush. The snow had piled into thicker drifts here, varying from eight or nine inches to a full two feet. We went down onto our knees and studied the spread beyond. It could have been a painting, for all that moved. Now that the wind had dropped, even the scraping, laddery windmill stood silent and still.

Ten minutes passed before we saw Lem step out of the barn, raise his New Model Sharps above his head and gesture that we should come in. We clambered to our feet, shoved through the brush and waded closer, leaving six jagged, white-grey scars to mark our passage.

When we were near enough, Lem said, "They' gone, cap'n. Cleared out. The woman as well." I did not know what to make of that. Lem went on, "From the looks of it, they ain't comin' back. Took ever'thin' they' likely to need." Then his eyes came up to mine and he said softly, "Only thing they left behind 'em wuz Bob Bancroft's hoss."

For a moment we all became part of the painting ourselves as we stood stock-still and pondered the implication of that. Then my eyes travelled past Lem to the house, with the cosy amber glow at its windows, and suddenly I pushed past him and went ploughing across the yard, stamped up onto the porch and shouldered the front door open.

I looked around. Nothing appeared to be amiss. I smelled cigarette smoke on the close, trapped air. Embers glowed in between the remnants of logs in the fireplace.

I went deeper into the room, my Yellow Boy at the ready. My voice was an intruder, breaking into the silence. "Bob?"

There came no response.

I took another few paces into the room, past a high-backed fireside chair. My foot snagged on something and, because I was so keyed-up, I swung around quickly, my finger whitening on the trigger.

I froze.

I had stumbled on an out-thrust leg. And slumped further back in the chair, staring right at me, sat Bob Bancroft.

My face crumpled into something full of anguish, and I mumbled, " . . . *no* . . . "

His shirt had been absolutely soaked in blood. Now, as it dried, it looked unnaturally stiff, like cardboard.

His throat had been cut.

I staggered away from him as the others came in through the front door. I turned away, dragged myself into the kitchen, bent over the sink and heaved.

Bancroft was dead. He had died as horrible a death as any man could. And all because of me.

Damn you, Kidd, I thought. *You're going to pay for this. You and all your men*. I forgot all about my hatred of killing. Right then I *wanted* to kill. I wanted to kill them *all*.

* * *

Bancroft's death left us stunned. I leaned over the sink, covered in sweat, trying to be sick even though I had nothing left in me to fetch up. I heard the other men mumbling expressions of their shock, heard the floorboards creak as they wandered around the room and tried to come to terms with what had happened.

I was weighed down by guilt. And why not? I had sent Bancroft to his death. Nobody else. I knew that my plan had never won the approval of the others, who had rightly seen the potential risks more clearly than I. So I must take full responsibility for it, and I did.

At last the feeling of nausea passed and I pushed myself erect. Quite by chance I caught sight of my reflection in a small looking-glass on the shelf at the bottom of the window. What I saw there shocked me still further.

Slowly I brought one hand up and let

my stiff fingers gently explore my face. But was that swollen, scabbed face really my own? Could the rigours of the hunt really have brought about such a drastic change in my appearance?

I peered closer, opened my mouth, tried to see inside it. As I had suspected, my tongue *had* swollen up, and the inside of my mouth looked sore and red.

I stood there for a moment, breathing shallowly. No wonder I had been feeling so terrible for so long. Finally I turned and went back to the others, but stopped before going into the parlour, where Bob Bancroft was still slumped in the chair, his throat a ragged crimson grimace.

The others turned to look at me. In somebody else's voice I said, "Wrap him in his blanket and take him home, boys. There's nothing more we can do here."

Still they stood there, watching me curiously. Nobody spoke. The breeze picked up suddenly, and the windmill started turning its ratchety cycle again. At length Saul said, "You sayin' we' not goin' after 'em, Mr Colter?"

"I'm saying that someone's got to take Bob home and see to it that he gets a proper burial," I replied.

"An' what 'bout Kidd?" asked Henry.

"What about Kidd?" I countered. "Even Lem here can't find tracks when they're buried under two feet of snow. Besides . . . " I cleared my throat behind a screening hand. "We can't go on riding together, boys. It's not safe."

They looked at me and I said, "I've got the small-pox."

I watched them react. Henry muttered, "Oh, Jesus," and Saul took an involuntary pace back. It was becoming a day for shocks and surprises.

I hadn't even wanted to admit it to myself. But I knew that I could no longer deny it, to myself or anyone else. Somewhere or other I had picked it up and now I was stuck with it. I could feel every scab and pus-filled sore on my face, around and inside my mouth, stippling my back and shoulders. It was only by some miracle that I did not appear to have infected my companions — but if they remained with me, it was only a matter of time.

Lem said, "Wal, speakin' fer myself, cap'n, I'd as soon not leave you to fend fer yourself. Not at a time like this."

"I appreciate that, Lem. But you men have an obligation to yourselves."

"We'll get you a doctor," said Saul. "Send one out from Overton."

I nodded, too weak to argue about it. "All right. If you can find one who'll come out in this weather." I made a loose gesture with one hand. "You'd better clear out of here and leave me to it."

They broke camp and fetched the horses in from the timber. Then they wrapped Bancroft in a blanket and tied him across his horse. I was careful to stay out of their way, all too aware now of the infectious nature of my illness. Snow started falling again, but it was a light sprinkling, and should not make their long journey back to town any more difficult than it already was.

At last they were ready to leave. I clung to the doorframe so that I could see them off.

"We'll fetch you a doctor, cap'n," Lem promised. "Get you well enough an' then we'll find that murderin' skunk an' string 'im up ourselfs."

It was fighting talk, I knew. We all wanted to find Kidd and make him pay for what he had done. But how were we to find him now? Winter had finally claimed the land, and it had come with a vengeance. And though none could have wanted him more than I, I could not help wondering if we would ever manage to run him to ground again.

9

WHEN they had gone, I closed the door and looked around the room. It seemed a lonely, miserable place for a man to die. With the last of my waning strength, I pushed the chair in which Bob Bancroft had died into the far corner, so that I would not have to look at it and be reminded of the man who had bled his life away upon it. Then I built up the fire and fell on to the lumpy, horsehair sofa and closed my eyes.

I slept, and woke up again sometime later in the day. I was fairly drenched with sweat. The fire had died down, so I built it up again. I stumbled into the kitchen and heaved into the sink, then crawled back on to the sofa and fell asleep once more.

My dreams were more like nightmares. I saw Ruth Buckhalter pointing one finger at me and shaking her head sorrowfully. I knew she was blaming me for Bancroft's death. Then he was there as well, and he was also jabbing an accusing finger at me and telling me that I never should have let it happen.

I saw Kansas Bill Johnson, bleeding from the bullet wound in his hip, threshing about beneath a threadbare blanket, begging to be allowed to rest.

Snow entered the weird landscape of my dream. But it wasn't snow that was drifting down from the heavens, it was dollar bills, ten thousand of them. That made me think of the ten thousand dollar bill in my pocket. Kidd started pointing at me then, adding his accusing finger to all the others.

Finally I woke up. It was pitch dark. I got up. I felt awful. A sudden gust of wind made the house creak. I dragged myself across to the window and peered outside. It was blowing a blizzard. I had never seen it snow so fiercely. Another gust of wind rocked the place. I hoped that the men were safe, that they had reached Overton by this time.

I turned around, fell down, crawled on my hands and knees to the hearth. I piled the last of the logs on to the embers and dug around with the poker to get a blaze going. Then I fell on to my side and dozed again, there on the floor.

I woke up next morning. It was still snowing. I tried to sit up but couldn't. Eventually I climbed back on to the sofa. My nose felt blocked, and I could not breathe through my mouth because of my swollen tongue.

Somehow the day passed. It stopped snowing. Some of the blisters around my mouth and across my shoulders burst. The fire went out. I had no more wood, and did not have the energy to go outside and fetch some.

The men had quartered my mustang in the barn. I hoped he was all right. It snowed again. I slept and woke up screaming. The house was like ice. I shivered, and wondered how long it would take for me to die.

Another night. I lay upon the floor, sweating and yet freezing as well. Outside, snow piled up. No doctor would be coming out here to tend to me now. I would die here, and that would be that.

I dozed, and somehow that night and most of the following day drifted past in a haze. Then, as afternoon was yielding to early evening, I finally felt the life ebbing out of me, and I knew with absolute certainty that I was dying.

I closed my eyes. Outside, the wind howled mournfully and pressed in on the freezing house. I heard snowflakes slapping at the windows and opened my eyes to watch the raging blizzard beyond the thick, distorted glass.

My eyelids drooped again. I felt myself beginning to drift, and I knew I was going to meet my Maker.

But then —

A footstep. Outside. The whicker of a cold horse.

My eyes flickered open again. I opened my mouth and tried to say, "In here!" but nothing came out, just a barely audible croak.

I held my breath, waiting. The door opened with a click. Wind and snow came inside. A man filled the doorway, in silhouette only. I looked up at him through glazed, suffering eyes. He closed the door behind him and looked down at me. I tried to lift one hand and beg him for help.

He came nearer. It was now very dark in the cold, cold house. Finally he knelt beside me and shook his head. "Look at the state of you, Colter," he said in mock reproof. "What are we going to do with you, eh?"

I saw him clearly then for the first time, and I could not believe my eyes. Surely I was dreaming again . . . for the newcomer was *John Kidd.*

★ ★ ★

Apparently heedless of the risk to himself, he got his arms under me and lifted me up onto the sofa. Then he went back outside to put up his horse. When next he came through the door, he was carrying a pile of logs in his arms. He built a fire, got it going, and when it began to spread its warmth through the room, he gave a satisfied nod.

Melting snow trickled down his thick pea jacket, and his well-defined face was reddened by exposure to the harsh wind. He took off his hat, which had been tied on with a scarf, threw it into a corner and ran one hand up through his flaxen hair.

It was then that I brought my .442 around on him and, with an almighty effort, thumbed back the hammer. "Take . . . take that C-Colt out and . . . throw it down here . . . beside me," I grunted. "Then . . . get your hands . . . up, you son-of-a-bitch. You . . . you're under . . . arrest."

He turned to look at me. There was

no surprise in his blue eyes, just an easy, assured touch of humour. "Put that gun down before someone gets hurt," he said, and then turned to head into the kitchen.

Overcome by fatigue, I let the gun drop to my side. It had taken all of my energy just to hold it up for thirty seconds. I listened to him moving about in the kitchen, firing up the range, searching in the cupboards for whatever supplies he and Ella might have left behind them.

Some time later he came back in and lit the lamp. The light hurt my eyes, and I tried to shield them. I noticed that he was holding a cup of water in his left hand. I was so thirsty by this time that I could hardly take my eyes off it. He came over, knelt beside me and held the cup to my lips. I gulped frantically. It was cold, and it made my teeth ache, but water, I thought, had never tasted so good.

"Well," he said conversationally. "It's a good thing I happened to hear of your misfortune, wasn't it?"

When I had emptied the cup, he stood up again, fished in his pocket and tossed a small, round tin into my lap. "Here, I fetched you some salve to dry up all those scabs. Rub some of it on, if you've got the strength. Then we'll see about getting some food inside you. We've got to build you up, Colter, otherwise you're going to die."

"Better you should . . . let me die . . . " I husked. "For if I live, I will . . . by-God . . . kill you, Kidd."

His face turned bleak. "For what happened to your men?" he asked.

I nodded.

His lips curled, and he shook his head in a kind of disgusted wonder. "Well, you hypocritical son-of-a-bitch," he said softly. "You can kill as many of *my* men as you like, and that's all right, because you think you've got justice on your side. But the minute you lose one of *your* men — "

"That's not the way of it, and you know it," I snapped, suddenly finding a new surge of life and spirit.

His eyebrows arched. "Isn't it, Colter? Oh, I'll confess that my men were not good men, not in the way that *you* would say they were good. But neither were they all bad. Circumstances put them on the path they followed. They weren't all as strong and high-minded as you. They gave *in* to temptation."

I frowned. This was a very different John Kidd to the one I had met that night in The Mother Lode. This one was older, more bitter and troubled. But in a perverse way, it pleased me to see some of the stuffing knocked out of him. "Don't presume to sit in judgement of me, Kidd," I warned him huskily.

"Oh, I wouldn't dare. But don't go acting so aggrieved because you lost a man — and not a very good man, if you want the truth of it — and expect me to accept the same thing without complaint just because it's one of the perils of my profession. We have feelings too, you know. We mourn our dead, just like everyone else."

I fixed him with a stern eye, completely unmoved. "I'll see that you pay for what you did to Bancroft," I grated. "My oath on it."

His response was another shake of the head. "For what *I* did?" he echoed. "Don't leave yourself out of it, Colter. It was your plan that got him killed. It was you who sent *him*, of all of them. Don't misunderstand me. He was your man, I know. But he was too sure of himself by half, that one. He had Ella fooled, I'll grant you. But not the rest of us. Not for one minute."

The warmth was chasing my chills away and I was beginning to revive somewhat. "So you . . . killed him. Stuck him . . . like a pig and let him . . . bleed to death."

"Shall I tell you something?" he asked, kneeling beside me again. "I've only ever killed one man in my life. I *detest* the act of killing, much as I've heard that you do. I saw my first man die when I was fourteen. His name was

Charley Craig and he was a friend of my granpaw's, a rustler.

"Well, not to beat around the bush, we were trying to lift some stock from a ranch up in Wyoming one time and the fellow who owned the place caught us in the act and let go with a scattergun. We lit out real fast, as you might imagine. But not before Charley Craig took most of that buckshot in the small of his back. I tell you, Colter, it fairly shredded his lungs.

"I watched him spitting up blood and gasping for breath for four days until he died. To this day, I'll never know how he lasted as long as he did. At the finish, he was begging us to put a bullet through his skull just to end his torment, but the others couldn't bring themselves to do it. But I did, because I wanted to help him. So I took Charley's own gun and levelled it at the side of his head and I splashed his brains all over Creation. That's a hell of a thing for a fourteen year-old to do, isn't it?"

He could not repress a shudder at the memory. "You've killed men," he said. "So you know what it's like. I promised myself there and then that I would never kill another man again, if I could help it. I've kept that promise."

"Sure," I said sarcastically.

He shrugged. "You can believe what you like, Colter. I'll stand by my record. I'm too interested in people to want to kill them. To my way of thinking, there's no good reason why larceny can't be civilised. Entertaining, even."

He rose up again. "Now, as far as your man was concerned, I was going to send him back to you. And if he hadn't made a damn'-fool play for his gun, I would have. But he tried to be a hero. He went for his Colt and Jim Middleton stuck him." He looked grey now. "That's why we lit out. Why we're going to split up. Because you can lift a man's cattle and steal his horses, you can rob banks and trains and celerity wagons, and the public will look upon you as a hero. But the minute you start killing — *everyone* wants to see you hang."

I frowned. "You . . . you're disbanding your gang?"

He nodded. "Uh-huh. But don't flatter yourself that it's all because of you — though I will confess, you've given me a run for my money." He grinned at that. "No. You're off this case now, Colter. The Cattlemen's Association has recalled you and your posse. The pursuit, apprehension and/or killing of John Kidd has now been taken out of your hands."

"*What?*"

"It's true. It seems I've upset more people than was wise for me. The American Bankers Association and Adams Express have hired Pinkerton's to run me to ground. And just to show that they mean business, they've posted a bounty of five thousand dollars on my head, and a thousand dollars each on those of my remaining men."

"So . . . so you're getting out," I

said. "While the getting's . . . good."

"Something like that."

I could not disguise my curiosity as I regarded him in the low, smoky lamp-light. "Why, Kidd?" I asked at last. "Why challenge me, I mean? Look how it's ended up."

Another gust of wind pushed at the house. He said, "I regret the death of your man, Colter. Hopefully you know that now. As to the why of it . . . Can't you guess?"

"Because . . . to you, all of this has just been . . . a game? Your wits against . . . mine?"

"There was more to it than that, my friend — although that was surely a part of it. And if you're half as sharp as I think you are, you'll work the rest of it out for yourself soon enough."

"Where . . . are you going?" I asked.

His smile suddenly stole years from his face. "That would be telling."

"Are you taking Ella with you?"

"Not only that. I'm going to make an honest woman of her, as well."

"Well . . . where . . . wherever you're going," I said, suddenly weakening again, "you'll need this." I felt in my pocket and brought out the ten thousand dollar note he had given me a lifetime before.

"Keep it," he replied easily. "It's of no value to me."

Suddenly his face grew troubled once more. He glanced at the blizzard beyond the window and shivered. "Now, you rub some of that salve onto your face while I go fix us something to eat, man. You look a fright the way you are right now."

He walked out into the kitchen, leaving me slumped there before the crackling fire, pondering everything he had told me.

* * *

With supplies he had fetched with him, Kidd fixed up some kind of a stew. I wish I could tell you it was good, but it wasn't. Still, it was hot and nourishing, and to a man who could no longer recall the last time he'd eaten, and whose creased and stained clothes now fell loosely upon him because of all the weight he'd lost, it was most welcome.

In fact, that meal remains one of the strangest experiences of my life. Even now I wonder if it were but an extension of my delirium. For there we sat, pursuer and pursued, breaking bread together in companionable silence, while snow piled up around us and the Arctic wind swiped at the house with enough force to make the windows rattle.

We were still on opposite sides of the fence. By rights, we should be fighting each other. And yet I did not feel the animosity towards him that I had. How could I, after all he had done for me?

At length I set my clean bowl down beside me and drifted back to sleep. The next time I woke it was daylight. A stack of logs had been piled neatly beside the fire. Steam was dribbling from the spout of a coffee pot before the hearth. There was a whole panful of stew still warm on the range. But of Kidd himself, there was no sign.

I had expected no less, of course. But still I felt lonelier for his having gone. I watched the bad weather through one of the windows and realised that my head was beginning to clear. I was not so stiff and achy. My tongue had returned to its normal size and my scabs were healing. I helped myself to some more of Kidd's awful stew throughout the course of the day, drank all the coffee and then found the energy to boil up some more.

The following morning I knew for certain that I was not going to die after all. The snow had stopped falling. The countryside was white, the sky grey, with the odd patch of blue. I shrugged into my jacket and jammed my hat down onto my head and went outside. The air was bracing, and it blew away the last of my cobwebs. I ploughed across to the barn and checked on my mustang. The horse was glad to see me. Kidd, I noted, had seen to his care.

I took my spare set of clothes from my saddlebags and hurried back to the house. There, I put a pan of water on to heat, stripped off, burned everything I had worn throughout my illness, then washed myself down. Within half an hour I was dressed again, this time in my spare white shirt and the black vest and trousers of my suit. That virtually completed the transformation in me.

I stayed at the ranch until I was sure the pox had gone. Two weeks later, there was a break in the weather and a sudden sweep of milder air up from the south thawed the worst of the snow. Seizing the opportunity, I saddled up and set off for town. I rode with much anticipation, for my self-imposed exile had been a long one. And yet a part of me had been renewed by the solitude of the ranch and the emptiness of the winter-locked land that surrounded it, and I was sorry to leave.

But there was still work to do — and I knew I could not hope to get on with my own life until it was completed.

★ ★ ★

About a month later I rode into Fort Wray and went to see Simon Black at his suite above the offices of the Fort Wray *Advocate*. He greeted me as effusively as ever and cheerfully paid me for all my efforts in trying to catch Kidd and put a stop to his rustling operation. In return I gave him three sealed envelopes. I knew I would not be seeing Lem, Saul or Henry again, and I wanted to make sure they knew just how much I had valued their companionship and assistance during our time together.

Black scanned the names on each of the envelopes and then nodded his balding head. "Never fear, Mr Colter," he said. "I will make sure these letters are delivered."

We chatted for a while, and then I

rose and we shook hands one final time and I left his office.

Downstairs, I paused for a moment on the boardwalk. It was early in the year 1878. Thanksgiving, Christmas and New Year were behind us, and the weather was slowly turning a gentler face towards us after the hardships of a savage winter.

I glanced to my right. I was curious about Kidd, and figured that I could probably satisfy that curiosity at the *Advocate*. Before I had taken more than a couple of steps, however, I was suddenly arrested by the sound of someone calling my name.

"*Colter!* Ash Colter!"

That voice. It made something twist in my stomach, and when I turned it was slowly, and with some trepidation.

Ruth Buckhalter was hurrying across the street towards me. I supposed she must have been in town on a rare shopping trip. She was wearing a heavy coat and a small, neat bonnet. Her smooth face was pale with the cold, and framed by lustrous dark blonde hair. Again I told myself that I had never knowingly entertained any romantic notions about her. And yet now, as I watched her hurry along the damp boardwalk with her full, ankle-length skirt bustling and shushing around her, I felt something else stir inside me — desire. I knew then that I wanted her, that I really, truly and in the purest way possible, *wanted* her.

She came to a halt and looked up into my face. She could not entirely hide her surprise at my appearance, for though I was no longer ill, I had stayed gaunt and pale.

I touched the brim of my hat cautiously and dipped my head. "Miss Buckhalter," I said by way of greeting. Then, remembering the invitation she had extended towards me all those months before. I amended it. "Ruth." And I smiled.

Her right hand blurred around and she slapped me across the face. It took me completely by surprise and snapped my head to one side. A few of the people hurrying this way or that along the boardwalk broke stride to look at us, then hurried on.

"That," she said in a low voice hoarsened by anger, "is for what you did to Bob Bancroft." She shook her head, and the expression on her beautiful face was one of disgust. "Yes, yes I heard all about what happened. How could you have done it, Colter? How could you have sent him into that . . . that den of thieves?" Tears came into her eyes and she shook her head some more. "It was your job, not his. It should have been *you* they killed, not him."

I said not a word. It wouldn't have done any good to try and explain the way of it to her. So I just stood there and took it, and if she decided she wanted to hit me again, I would let her take another swing, if it made her feel any better.

She didn't though. She just said, "It should have been you," again, then

240

turned on her heel and hurried away, one hand up to her face and a sob breaking in her throat.

★ ★ ★

I tried to push her from my mind, although I am bound to say that it wasn't easy. But I still had work to do.

I went into the *Advocate* office and asked to look through whatever clippings they had on John Kidd. The clerk looked at me curiously. Perhaps he knew me by sight or reputation. Perhaps he'd seen what had just happened out on the street. Whichever, he finally nodded and showed me to a spare desk, and then went away to fetch a fairly bulky folder.

I opened it and started reading. It soon proved to be a very sorry story.

Kidd and the remaining members of his gang had agreed to each go their separate ways. But before they could do that, they needed money. So they set about trying to steal some.

On December 12, they had tried to rob a train. They had piled ties on some tracks just outside St Paul, Nebraska, and stopped the twelve o'clock eastbound. Then they blasted open the mail car and ordered the startled young messenger to open the safe.

The messenger refused.

Kidd jabbed his pistol into the young man's face and told him he'd better do as he was told, or else.

Still the messenger refused.

There was some talk of shooting him in the legs unless he cooperated. To their complete surprise, however, the feisty messenger told them to go ahead and do their worst.

That was when a truly remarkable thing happened.

Kidd pushed his men down to the far end of the car. He spoke earnestly for thirty seconds. There was some argument from Preacher Sweet and Jim Middleton, who were all for killing the messenger and blowing the safe with dynamite. But when Kidd finally came back down to the young man, it was merely to offer him that famous, easy smile and compliment him on his courage.

Then, even more remarkably, the outlaws climbed down from the train, went back up the tracks, removed the ties and allowed the train to go on its way.

They had better luck up in Dakota Territory, where they stole eight thousand dollars from the paymaster in a goldmining camp along the Big Sioux River. But in their rush to out-run the hastily-convened posse that soon came after them, Dutch Arnie Bakke dropped a bag of silver and reduced their take by two thousand five hundred dollars.

After that, things went from bad to worse.

The way it read, Kidd and his gang had been chased right across the country, for Pinkerton's had increased the rewards by five hundred dollars per man and, in Kidd's case, by an extra two and a half thousand.

There was no doubt about it. For Kidd and his men, the writing was on the wall. With so much money on offer, every man with a pistol would be keeping his eyes peeled and looking to make his fortune. From now on, it was only a matter of time.

I was right.

The remainder of the clippings were a catalogue of disaster for the outlaws. Killin' Jim Middleton was caught and killed when he tried to cash a stolen Adams Express note in Madison, Minnesota. Tiburcio Mendez was arrested at a gaming house in Topeka, Kansas. Dutch Arnie Bakke came down with appendicitis in Wichita and was recognised by the doctor who came to treat him. After the operation, he woke up to find himself handcuffed to his bed, and under armed guard. And finally, Preacher Sweet was cornered after a failed bank robbery in Perryton, down in the Texas Panhandle, and shot dead.

That just left Kidd.

Kidd.

As I closed the folder, I wondered what his and Ella's life had become. One endless pursuit, more than likely. I wondered what it must be like to be hounded, hunted, chased, stalked, tracked so relentlessly, and concluded that it must be a nightmare.

Again I felt the outline of the ten thousand dollar bill in my pocket. If that was what Kidd's life had become, then my own course of action was clear. I had to find him and end it, once and for all.

I must kill John Kidd, and end the endless pursuit forever.

10

I SENT a confidential wire to Allan Pinkerton, the founder and general superintendent of Pinkerton's National Detective Agency, in care of his head office in Chicago, expressing my desire to help in the apprehension or elimination of John Kidd. I made much of my previous experience in law-enforcement as well as my association with Jack Page, and said that I had learned much about Kidd during our recent skirmishes in Colorado and Kansas that might prove instrumental in finally bringing him to justice.

For the first time in my life, I was glad I had the reputation I did, for now I felt that it might work *for* me, and open doors that would otherwise remain firmly shut.

Three days later a boy fetched a return wire to my hotel room. Eagerly

246

I tore it open and scanned the contents. It was from Pinkerton himself. He said he had heard of me, and would be happy to discuss the matter of John Kidd at much greater length in person. Therefore, would I hasten to Chicago as quickly as possible.

It was a hellish distance to request a man to travel — some seven hundred and fifty miles. But I did not think he would have asked me if he did not want me to be a part of Kidd's eventual downfall.

I will not delay you with details of the long and often tedious train journey across Kansas and Iowa to Illinois. Suffice it to say that, just over a week later, I arrived at bustling 5th Avenue and was shown up to the offices of the great man.

I was shocked when I saw him, for though I knew he was a sick man, I was not prepared for the extent of his illness. He was not yet sixty, but looking at him now, I would have put him closer to eighty. He had suffered a 'shock', or stroke, nearly a decade earlier, and it had left him partially crippled and unable to speak with any great clarity. Yet still he worked half-days at the office, overseeing all the affairs of his great concern.

He bade me enter and take a seat across the desk from him. He asked me to tell him all that I knew of Kidd, and seemed impressed with my reply.

His son Robert was there with him, and he did much of his father's talking for him. He confided that their employers in the matter, the highly influential American Bankers Association, as well as Adams Express, were baying for Kidd's blood. They wanted his head on a plate, and Pinkerton's was honour-bound to give it to them.

"All our sources now indicate that Kidd fled down to New Orleans," he went on, standing by the large window and looking down at the concrete metropolis below. "He bought passage for himself and a woman named Ella

Morris aboard a steamer and sailed south. Now, after much painstaking investigation, we believe we have finally located him down in Colonia, where he is in the process of establishing a beef-exporting business under the name of Childs."

I frowned. "Colonia? Where's that, down in Mexico?"

"Just outside Buenos Aires," Robert replied. "That's in Argentina."

Argentina! Geography had never been my strong point, but even *I* knew that Argentina was thousands of miles away. Kidd was unreachable there. He had managed to out-distance his pursuers after all.

But I was wrong about that.

"We are planning to send a delegation down there to bring him back to stand trial in the United States," Robert said, coming back over to resume his seat to one side of the big desk. "We have no reason to suspect that the Argentinian authorities will refuse the extradition. But if Kidd himself puts up a fight, our orders are equally clear — he's got to pay for his crimes, one way or the other. It makes no difference to us."

"How big a delegation are you proposing to send?" I enquired.

"We haven't decided yet. Ever since that business with McParland and the Mollie Maguires some years ago, my father has preferred not to assign too many operatives to any one case, and I'm inclined to agree with him. Too many men and Kidd might be forewarned."

Reaching a swift, impulsive decision, I drew in a deep breath and said, "I'll go down there and bring him back for you."

Old Allan stirred in his chair and fixed his watery but still sharp eyes upon me. "Alone?" he slurred.

"I think that's best," I replied.

He thought about it for a moment. After a while he glanced at his son. Robert nodded and said, "Mr Colter, we were hoping you would volunteer for the task. We are, of course very familiar with your enviable reputation, and are of the opinion that if any man can do it — you can."

Thus it was settled.

* * *

It took me two months and four thousand miles to reach my destination. First of all I travelled by rail to Pascagoula, Mississippi, and caught a tramp steamer south across the Gulf of Mexico and on into the Caribbean. We docked in Columbia and I hired a little peasant with a face the same colour and texture as a walnut to take me down through the steamy jungles to Buenaventura. There I bought passage on another steamer that regularly plied the coastlines of Ecuador, Peru and Chile.

The captain packed more and more men, women, children, chickens, goats, pigs and dogs aboard at every port of call. I marvelled at the fact that the boat did not sink beneath our combined weight. But the Pacific was as calm as its name suggested, and I had plenty of time to think, and question the wisdom of my undertaking.

It was a relief when we finally chugged into the crowded dock at Valparaiso sometime in the middle of April, for I knew that most of the journey was behind me at last. A railway service of sorts connected the noisy, bustling city with Buenos Aires, some seven hundred-odd miles to the east, and I squeezed myself aboard the first clanking, rocking train out.

We travelled through vast tracts of lush, damp jungle. On five separate occasions the train broke down and the passengers — easily more than a thousand of us — had to climb down and kill time until the engine could be patched up or replaced. I sweated pints in the humid air. Everything I ate seemed to disagree with me. But in due course I crossed Argentina from one side to the other and finally, finally, I reached Buenos Aires.

The city was situated on the westernmost shore of a broad muddy estuary known as the Rio de la Plata. On the day I arrived, the humid weather knocked me back on my heels. Never before had I seen such a metropolis. It was a tightly-packed jumble of fine stone town-houses and mean, cramped little shacks and tenements. Everywhere I looked there were people of all nationalities, as well as a goodly proportion of dark-skinned *mestizos*.

According to the information Robert Pinkerton had given me, Kidd's ranch lay some fifty miles to the north. Eager to get this business over and done with, I rented a horse and mule at a stable on the Avenida Paseo Colon, bought some supplies and set off later that same afternoon.

The countryside was largely fea-tureless, mostly flat, grassy plains. Patches of marshland nestled in shallow swells. The odd scattering of thorn thickets and *guebrachos* did their best to break the monotony, as did the smoky blue bulks of the distant *sierras*, but to my mind it was a vast, lonely and frankly bleak land.

I camped that evening in the shade of some palm savannas and cooked a meal. By my reckoning, I would reach Kidd's place early on the morrow. Just the thought of it was enough to make my pulses beat faster, my throat tighten and dry up, my stomach clench.

I slept in fits and starts that night, and when I woke up a little before dawn the following morning, there was a heavy sense of dread inside me. Unable to face food, I washed, boiled and drank some coffee, then broke camp, saddled up and rode on north.

About two hours later, with the sun a massive crimson ball edging slowly up over the eastern horizon, I saw the first of Kidd's cattle, big, heavy-set creatures scattered right across the *pampas*, chewing lazily on the rich grass as they watched me through disinterested eyes and twitched their ears occasionally to shoo away the flies.

The sun lifted higher and the day started to break. Sweat slid down my flushed face and dampened my shirt at the armpits and the small of the back.

Half an hour later, the ranch itself came into sight.

I slowed the rented horse and studied the place. In the faintly orange light of early morning it looked quiet, just a couple of low frame buildings and sheds, a few carefully-planted shade trees and a corral in which horses were already rolling and frolicking.

According to the information Robert Pinkerton had managed to gather, Kidd employed three *vaqueros*. I dismounted whilst still two or three hundred yards out, and waited until I saw them leave the ranch to begin the day's work. Then I mounted up again and clucked my horse and mule into movement.

Chickens were clucking and strutting before the house when I rode in. Smoke was rising from the stone chimney in little grey streamers, a sign that breakfast was being cooked. A man was washing up in the trough out front of the house. He was stripped to the waist, leaning forward and dunking his head into the cold water. He had his back to me, and so was not aware of my approach.

I walked the horse into the yard and reined down twenty feet away from him. He dunked his head again, then brought it back up. Water streamed off him like molten silver, and I watched his shoulders heave as he gulped for air.

I watched him for a moment longer, not trusting myself to speak immediately. Finally I swallowed hard, licked my lips and called down, "Kidd."

His shoulders stiffened, and the tracery of muscles beneath his berry-brown skin suddenly bunched. He did not make any other move, though, just stood there with his back to me, trying to place my voice, waiting to see what happened next.

What happened next was that I told him to turn around, which he did, slowly.

He had not changed, save to fill out a little. Life out here had evidently been good for him, I thought. I looked into his face. It was tight with suspicion and surprise and dismay. Water was still streaming down it from beneath his glistening flaxen hair.

At last he opened his mouth and said, "My God. Colter."

I could imagine what kind of a shock it must have been for him, but he bore it well. He was unarmed, so I chanced a brief look away from him, and concentrated my attention on the rest of the place. It was much bigger and better-kept than the ranch down along the Saline.

When he spoke again, I returned my gaze to him. "I . . . I suppose I can guess what's brought you all this way," he said carefully.

I nodded. "The Pinkertons tracked you down, John. They know you're here. They know all about this beef-exporting business you're trying to set up. They sent me to fetch you back to stand trial."

His lip curled.

"You must have known someone would come for you sooner or later," I said.

He nodded bitterly. "Yes," he replied, reaching up slowly to push his wet hair back off his face. "Yes, I guess I did. It's always been a fear, but not so much for me, for Ella." He looked up at me again, one eye closed against the building sunlight. "Is that why you're here, then, Colter? To . . . take me back?"

I shook my head. "Not to take you back, no."

"Then . . . what . . . ?"

The blood drained from his face and his mouth dropped open as he supplied his own answer. He brought his hands up as though to ward me off, and he opened his mouth to make some sort of protest, but before he could say anything a gunshot crashed through the dawn and, startled, my horse reared up on to its hind legs and I fell backwards and slammed against the packed dirt of the yard with sufficient force to knock the wind from my sails.

My horse and the pack mule danced sideways. Another gunshot rang out. Dirt sprayed into my face and got into my eyes. I rolled sideways, came up, drew my gun from leather and yelled, *"All right, that's enough!"*

I focused on the newcomer then. It was Ella Morris — Ella Kidd or Childs as she now was — standing on the porch of the house, a smoking Winchester in her hands, a look of indescribable anguish on her face as she struggled to fetch the long gun up on me again.

I shouted, *"Put it down, Ella! Put — the — gun down!"* And Kidd, who had turned at the waist, as surprised as I, added his own encouragement. "Do it, Ella! For God's sake, put the gun down . . . "

She held back for a moment, not sure what to do. She whispered, "B-but he s-said . . . I heard him . . . he's going to *kill* you, John . . . "

Kidd went over to her, took the rifle away and threw it into the dust with an air of finality. I noticed then that Ella was pregnant, that she was about midway through her confinement. "All right!" Kidd snapped. "So he's going to kill me! Better that than carry on the way we have, always looking over our shoulders, just waiting for them to catch up with us!"

"J-John . . . "

"Better I should die here and have done with it," he went on, unable to stem his sour flow now, "than go back home and face *his* idea of justice!" He turned to me then, and his blue eyes were alight with hatred. "Still, I'm surprised that you should be the one, Colter. I always felt there was some kinship between us, that you were different to all the rest, that you *understood*."

I went a couple of paces forward, my gun hanging loosely at my side. The worry and desperation on each of their faces was a pitiful thing to see. I said, "They're out for your blood back home, John. One way or the other, you *have* to die."

He looked me right in the eye. "Best you get on with it, then," he grunted. "Damn you."

I raised my gun, thumbed back the hammer, took aim. Ella whispered tremulously, "N-no . . . "

I fired the gun, sending a shot into the sky that made them both flinch.

"There," I said, pouching the weapon again. "It's done."

Kidd, holding Ella now, frowned at me. "Wh . . . what . . . what k-kind of a game is it you're playing here, Colter?"

I said, "I came out here to arrest John Kidd. I wanted to do it peaceably, but he made a fight of it. We exchanged shots. I got lucky. He died."

There was a long silence then, as

261

they both sifted all the implications of what my lie was offering them. No more pursuit. No more watching and waiting, no more uncertainty, no more dread. *Ever.*

Licking his lips, almost afraid to believe it, Kidd looked me in the eye, his brows lowered in a frown. "You . . . came all this way," he said in a soft, slightly baffled voice. "To do *this* for *me?*"

I nodded.

"Why?"

Hoofbeats rolled across the *pampas* before I could answer. Kidd's *vaqueros* were coming back in, alerted by all the gunfire. Ella came down off the porch and shuffled out to meet them and tell them that everything was fine. Kidd came down with her, let her go and stood before me, his eyes searching and unsure.

"Do you think it will work?" he asked. "That they'll believe you when you get back to Chicago?"

I had thought long and hard about

that. Now I nodded. Of course it would work. I was Ash Colter. *The* Ash Colter. I would give them my word on the truth of it, and they would accept it without question, because in those days a man's word carried a lot more weight than it does now.

"They'll believe," I said.

His relief was obvious in the sudden slump of his shoulders.

We shook hands.

Ella came back over then, ungainly in her pregnancy. Behind us, the *vaqueros* turned their horses and rode back out to tend the cattle.

I looked down at her. She was looking back up at me in that strangely direct way she had. After a while, convinced of my sincerity, she allowed a smile to brush at the corners of her mouth and impulsively reached out to take one of my arms and squeeze it.

"Thank you," she said hoarsely. "Thank you for letting my child keep his father."

I shuffled my feet.

"You'll stay for a while," Kidd said.

"Well, I'll stay for breakfast."

"That's not what I mean," he replied. "You'd be more than welcome, for there's still plenty to do here before this place is completely up and running, and I can use the help of a good, reliable man."

I held back from committing myself.

"Think about it," he said. "Go put your animals up in the barn while Ella sets another place for breakfast and I go put on a shirt."

I went and gathered up the reins and dragged my horse and mule into the cool shadows of the barn. For the first time in my life, I felt good about who I was and what life had made of me. I had come to terms with myself here today, and I had settled my debts. For in the end I had owed John Kidd far more than I had ever thought it possible to repay.

When he had thrown down the gauntlet to me that night in The Mother Lode, I had been aching with the guilt of Dick Mills' death. Kidd's challenge had given me a purpose, had made me pull myself together.

Then, as time wore on, he had made me realise that there was good and bad in everyone, that no one man or woman was all one thing or the other, but rather a mixture of the two.

I owed him because he had saved my life that night when I had felt sure that the smallpox was going to kill me.

And most of all, I owed him a debt of thanks because today he had given me a chance to use my gun to *give* a life, instead of take it.

I off-saddled the animals and turned them out into the corral, listening to the gentle sounds of the ranch at work, and thinking about Kidd's invitation.

I was facing a long journey home. I could use a reviving week or two here, before I began my return to America.

I unbuckled my gun, coiled the belt around the holster and tucked the whole into my saddlebag. There was no need of the weapon here now. And perhaps never again.

I stepped back out into the strong Argentinian sunshine and went to get some breakfast.

THE END

FIGHTING RAMROD
Charles N. Heckelmann

Most men would have cut their losses, but Frazer counted the bullets in his guns and said he'd soak the range in blood before he'd give up another inch of what was his.

LONE GUN
Eric Allen

Smoke Blackbird had been away too long. The Lequires had seized the Blackbird farm, forcing the Indians and settlers off, and no one seemed willing to fight! He had to fight alone.

THE THIRD RIDER
Barry Cord

Mel Rawlins wasn't going to let anything stand in his way. His father was murdered, his two brothers gone. Now Mel rode for vengeance.

ARIZONA DRIFTERS
W. C. Tuttle

When drifting Dutton and Lonnie Steelman decide to become partners they find that they have a common enemy in the formidable Thurston brothers.

TOMBSTONE
Matt Braun

Wells Fargo paid Luke Starbuck to outgun the silver-thieving stagecoach gang at Tombstone. Before long Luke can see the only thing bearing fruit in this eldorado will be the gallows tree.

HIGH BORDER RIDERS
Lee Floren

Buckshot McKee and Tortilla Joe cut the trail of a border tough who was running Mexican beef into Texas. They stopped the smuggler in his tracks.

BRETT RANDALL, GAMBLER
E. B. Mann

Larry Day had the choice of running away from the law or of assuming a dead man's place. No matter what he decided he was bound to end up dead.

THE GUNSHARP
William R. Cox

The Eggerleys weren't very smart. They trained their sights on Will Carney and Arizona's biggest blood bath began.

THE DEPUTY OF SAN RIANO
Lawrence A. Keating and
Al. P. Nelson

When a man fell dead from his horse, Ed Grant was spotted riding away from the scene. The deputy sheriff rode out after him and came up against everything from gunfire to dynamite.

FARGO: MASSACRE RIVER
John Benteen

The ambushers up ahead had now blocked the road. Fargo's convoy was a jumble, a perfect target for the insurgents' weapons!

SUNDANCE: DEATH IN THE LAVA
John Benteen

The Modoc's captured the wagon train and its cargo of gold. But now the halfbreed they called Sundance was going after it . . .

HARSH RECKONING
Phil Ketchum

Five years of keeping himself alive in a brutal prison had made Brand tough and careless about who he gunned down . . .

FARGO: PANAMA GOLD
John Benteen

With foreign money behind him, Buckner was going to destroy the Panama Canal before it could be completed. Fargo's job was to stop Buckner.

FARGO:
THE SHARPSHOOTERS
John Benteen

The Canfield clan, thirty strong were raising hell in Texas. Fargo was tough enough to hold his own against the whole clan.

PISTOL LAW
Paul Evan Lehman

Lance Jones came back to Mustang for just one thing — revenge! Revenge on the people who had him thrown in jail.

HELL RIDERS
Steve Mensing

Wade Walker's kid brother, Duane, was locked up in the Silver City jail facing a rope at dawn. Wade was a ruthless outlaw, but he was smart, and he had vowed to have his brother out of jail before morning!

DESERT OF THE DAMNED
Nelson Nye

The law was after him for the murder of a marshal — a murder he didn't commit. Breen was after him for revenge — and Breen wouldn't stop at anything . . . blackmail, a frameup . . . or murder.

DAY OF THE COMANCHEROS
Steven C. Lawrence

Their very name struck terror into men's hearts — the Comancheros, a savage army of cutthroats who swept across Texas, leaving behind a bloodstained trail of robbery and murder.

SUNDANCE: SILENT ENEMY
John Benteen

A lone crazed Cheyenne was on a personal war path. They needed to pit one man against one crazed Indian. That man was Sundance.

LASSITER
Jack Slade

Lassiter wasn't the kind of man to listen to reason. Cross him once and he'll hold a grudge for years to come — if he let you live that long.

LAST STAGE TO GOMORRAH
Barry Cord

Jeff Carter, tough ex-riverboat gambler, now had himself a horse ranch that kept him free from gunfights and card games. Until Sturvesant of Wells Fargo showed up.

McALLISTER ON THE COMANCHE CROSSING
Matt Chisholm

The Comanche, McAllister owes them a life — and the trail is soaked with the blood of the men who had tried to outrun them before.

QUICK-TRIGGER COUNTRY
Clem Colt

Turkey Red hooked up with Curly Bill Graham's outlaw crew. But wholesale murder was out of Turk's line, so when range war flared he bucked the whole border gang alone . . .

CAMPAIGNING
Jim Miller

Ambushed on the Santa Fe trail, Sean Callahan is saved by two Indian strangers. But there'll be more lead and arrows flying before the band join Kit Carson against the Comanches.

GUNSLINGER'S RANGE
Jackson Cole

Three escaped convicts are out for revenge. They won't rest until they put a bullet through the head of the dirty snake who locked them behind bars.

RUSTLER'S TRAIL
Lee Floren

Jim Carlin knew he would have to stand up and fight because he had staked his claim right in the middle of Big Ike Outland's best grass.

THE TRUTH ABOUT SNAKE RIDGE
Marshall Grover

The troubleshooters came to San Cristobal to help the needy. For Larry and Stretch the turmoil began with a brawl and then an ambush.

WOLF DOG RANGE
Lee Floren

Will Ardery would stop at nothing, unless something stopped him first — like a bullet from Pete Manly's gun.

DEVIL'S DINERO
Marshall Grover

Plagued by remorse, a rich old reprobate hired the Texas Troubleshooters to deliver a fortune in greenbacks to each of his victims.

GUNS OF FURY
Ernest Haycox

Dane Starr, alias Dan Smith, wanted to close the door on his past and hang up his guns, but people wouldn't let him.

DONOVAN
Elmer Kelton

Donovan was supposed to be dead. Uncle Joe Vickers had fired off both barrels of a shotgun into the vicious outlaw's face as he was escaping from jail. Now Uncle Joe had been shot — in just the same way.

CODE OF THE GUN
Gordon D. Shirreffs

MacLean came riding home, with saddle tramp written all over him, but sewn in his shirt-lining was an Arizona Ranger's star.

GAMBLER'S GUN LUCK
Brett Austen

Gamblers seldom live long. Parker was a hell of a gambler. It was his life — or his death . . .

ORPHAN'S PREFERRED
Jim Miller

Sean Callahan answers the call of the Pony Express and fights Indians and outlaws to get the mail through.

DAY OF THE BUZZARD
T. V. Olsen

All Val Penmark cared about was getting the men who killed his wife.

THE MANHUNTER
Gordon D. Shirreffs

Lee Kershaw knew that every Rurale in the territory was on the lookout for him. But the offer of $5,000 in gold to find five small pieces of leather was too good to turn down.

RIFLES ON THE RANGE
Lee Floren

Doc Mike and the farmer stood there alone between Smith and Watson. There was this moment of stillness, and then the roar would start. And somebody would die . . .

HARTIGAN
Marshall Grover

Hartigan had come to Cornerstone to die. He chose the time and the place, and Main Street became a battlefield.

SUNDANCE: OVERKILL
John Benteen

When a wealthy banker's daughter was kidnapped by the Cheyenne, he offered Sundance $10,000 to rescue the girl.